A FAMILY

Maupassant Original Short Stories

Volume XI

Guy de Maupassant

iBoo Press
London

A FAMILY

Maupasant Original Short Stories

Volume XI

Guy de Maupassant

Translated by
ALBERT M. C. McMASTER, B.A.
A. E. HENDERSON, B.A.
MME. QUESADA and Others

Layout & Cover © Copyright 2020 iBooPress, London

Published by
iBoo Press House

3rd Floor
86-90 Paul Street
London, EC2A4NE UK

t: +44 20 3695 0809
info@iboo.com II iBoo.com

ISBN
978-1-64181-749-3 (p)

Printed in the United States

A FAMILY

Maupasant Original Short Stories

Volume XI

Guy de Maupassant

A FAMILY

VOLUME XI

THE UMBRELLA

*M*me. Oreille was a very economical woman; she knew the value of a centime, and possessed a whole storehouse of strict principles with regard to the multiplication of money, so that her cook found the greatest difficulty in making what the servants call their market-penny, and her husband was hardly allowed any pocket money at all. They were, however, very comfortably off, and had no children; but it really pained Mme. Oreille to see any money spent; it was like tearing at her heartstrings when she had to take any of those nice crown-pieces out of her pocket; and whenever she had to spend anything, no matter how necessary it might be, she slept badly the next night.

Oreille was continually saying to his wife:

"You really might be more liberal, as we have no children, and never spend our income."

"You don't know what may happen," she used to reply. "It is better to have too much than too little."

She was a little woman of about forty, very active, rather hasty, wrinkled, very neat and tidy, and with a very short temper.

Her husband frequently complained of all the privations she made him endure; some of them were particularly painful to him, as they touched his vanity.

He was one of the head clerks in the War Office, and only stayed on there in obedience to his wife's wish, to increase their income which they did not nearly spend.

For two years he had always come to the office with the same old patched umbrella, to the great amusement of his fellow clerks. At last he got tired of their jokes, and insisted upon his wife buying him a new one. She bought one for eight francs and a half, one of those cheap articles which large houses sell as an advertisement. When the men in the office saw the article, which was being sold in Paris by the thousand, they began their jokes again, and Oreille had a dreadful time of it. They even made a song about it, which he heard from morning till night all over the immense building.

Oreille was very angry, and peremptorily told his wife to get him a new one, a good silk one, for twenty francs, and to bring him the bill, so that he might see that it was all right.

She bought him one for eighteen francs, and said, getting red with anger as she gave it to her husband:

"This will last you for five years at least."

Oreille felt quite triumphant, and received a small ovation at the office with his new acquisition.

When he went home in the evening his wife said to him, looking at the umbrella uneasily:

"You should not leave it fastened up with the elastic; it will very likely cut the silk. You must take care of it, for I shall not buy you a new one in a hurry."

She took it, unfastened it, and remained dumfounded with astonishment and rage; in the middle of the silk there was a hole as big as a six-penny-piece; it had been made with the end of a cigar.

"What is that?" she screamed.

Her husband replied quietly, without looking at it:

"What is it? What do you mean?"

She was choking with rage, and could hardly get out a word.

"You—you—have—burned—your umbrella! Why—you must be—mad! Do you wish to ruin us outright?"

He turned round, and felt that he was growing pale.

"What are you talking about?"

"I say that you have burned your umbrella. Just look here."

And rushing at him, as if she were going to beat him, she violently thrust the little circular burned hole under his nose.

He was so utterly struck dumb at the sight of it that he could only stammer out:

"What-what is it? How should I know? I have done nothing, I will swear. I don't know what is the matter with the umbrella."

"You have been playing tricks with it at the office; you have been playing the fool and opening it, to show it off!" she screamed.

"I only opened it once, to let them see what a nice one it was, that is all, I swear."

But she shook with rage, and got up one of those conjugal scenes which make a peaceable man dread the domestic hearth more than a battlefield where bullets are raining.

She mended it with a piece of silk cut out of the old umbrella, which was of a different color, and the next day Oreille went off very humbly with the mended article in his hand. He put it into a cupboard, and thought no more of it than of some unpleasant recollection.

But he had scarcely got home that evening when his wife took the umbrella from him, opened it, and nearly had a fit when she saw what had befallen it, for the disaster was irreparable. It was covered with small holes, which evidently proceeded from burns, just as if some one had emptied the ashes from a lighted pipe on to it. It was done for utterly, irreparably.

She looked at it without a word, in too great a passion to be able to say anything. He, also, when he saw the damage, remained almost dumfounded, in a state of frightened consternation.

They looked at each other, then he looked at the floor; and the next moment she threw the useless article at his head, screaming out in a transport of the most violent rage, for she had recovered her voice by that time:

"Oh! you brute! you brute! You did it on purpose, but I will pay you out for it. You shall not have another."

And then the scene began again, and after the storm had raged for an hour, he at last was able to explain himself. He declared that he could not understand it at all, and that it could only proceed from malice or from vengeance.

A ring at the bell saved him; it was a friend whom they were expecting to dinner.

Mme. Oreille submitted the case to him. As for buying a new umbrella, that was out of the question; her husband should not have another. The friend very sensibly said that in that case his clothes would be spoiled, and they were certainly worth more than the umbrella. But the little woman, who was still in a rage, replied:

"Very well, then, when it rains he may have the kitchen umbrella, for I will not give him a new silk one."

Oreille utterly rebelled at such an idea.

"All right," he said; "then I shall resign my post. I am not going to the office with the kitchen umbrella."

The friend interposed.

"Have this one re-covered; it will not cost much."

But Mme. Oreille, being in the temper that she was, said:

"It will cost at least eight francs to re-cover it. Eight and eighteen are twenty-six. Just fancy, twenty-six francs for an umbrella! It is utter madness!"

The friend, who was only a poor man of the middle classes, had an inspiration:

"Make your fire assurance pay for it. The companies pay for all articles that are burned, as long as the damage has been done in your own house."

On hearing this advice the little woman calmed down immediately, and then, after a moment's reflection, she said to her husband:

"To-morrow, before going to your office, you will go to the Maternelle Assurance Company, show them the state your umbrella is in, and make them pay for the damage."

M. Oreille fairly jumped, he was so startled at the proposal.

"I would not do it for my life! It is eighteen francs lost, that is all. It will not ruin us."

The next morning he took a walking-stick when he went out, and, luckily, it was a fine day.

Left at home alone, Mme. Oreille could not get over the loss of her eighteen francs by any means. She had put the umbrella on the dining-room table, and she looked at it without being able to come to any determination.

Every moment she thought of the assurance company, but she did not dare to encounter the quizzical looks of the gentlemen who might receive her, for she was very timid before people, and blushed at a mere nothing, and was embarrassed when she had to speak to strangers.

But the regret at the loss of the eighteen francs pained her as if she had been wounded. She tried not to think of it any more, and yet every moment the recollection of the loss struck her painfully. What was she to do, however? Time went on, and she could not decide; but suddenly, like all cowards, on making a resolve, she became determined.

"I will go, and we will see what will happen."

But first of all she was obliged to prepare the umbrella so that the disaster might be complete, and the reason of it quite evident. She took a match from the mantelpiece, and between the ribs she burned a hole as big as the palm of her hand; then she delicately rolled it up, fastened it with the elastic band, put on her bonnet and shawl, and went quickly toward the Rue de Rivoli, where the assurance office was.

But the nearer she got, the slower she walked. What was she going to say, and what reply would she get?

She looked at the numbers of the houses; there were still twenty-eight. That was all right, so she had time to consider, and she walked slower and slower. Suddenly she saw a door on which was a large brass plate with "La Maternelle Fire Assurance Office" engraved on it. Already! She waited a moment, for she felt nervous and almost ashamed; then she walked past, came back, walked past again, and came back again.

At last she said to herself:

"I must go in, however, so I may as well do it sooner as later."

She could not help noticing, however, how her heart beat as she entered. She went into an enormous room with grated doors all round it, and above them little openings at which a man's head appeared, and as a gentleman carrying a number of papers passed her, she stopped him and said timidly: "I beg your pardon, monsieur, but can you tell me where I must apply for payment for anything that has been accidentally burned?"

He replied in a sonorous voice:

"The first door on the left; that is the department you want."

This frightened her still more, and she felt inclined to run away, to put in no claim, to sacrifice her eighteen francs. But the idea of that sum revived her courage, and she went upstairs, out of breath, stopping at almost every other step.

She knocked at a door which she saw on the first landing, and a clear voice said, in answer:

"Come in!"

She obeyed mechanically, and found herself in a large room where three solemn gentlemen, all with a decoration in their buttonholes, were standing talking.

One of them asked her: "What do you want, madame?"

She could hardly get out her words, but stammered: "I have come—I have come on account of an accident, something—".

He very politely pointed out a seat to her,

"If you will kindly sit down I will attend to you in a moment."

And, returning to the other two, he went on with the conversation.

"The company, gentlemen, does not consider that it is under any obligation to you for more than four hundred thousand francs, and we can pay no attention to your claim to the further sum of a hundred thousand, which you wish to make us pay. Besides that, the surveyor's valuation—"

One of the others interrupted him:

"That is quite enough, monsieur; the law courts will decide between us, and we have nothing further to do than to take our leave." And they went out after mutual ceremonious bows.

Oh! if she could only have gone away with them, how gladly she would have done it; she would have run away and given up everything. But it was too late, for the gentleman came back, and said, bowing:

"What can I do for you, madame?"

She could scarcely speak, but at last she managed to say:

"I have come-for this."

The manager looked at the object which she held out to him in mute astonishment.

With trembling fingers she tried to undo the elastic, and succeeding, after several attempts, she hastily opened the damaged remains of the umbrella.

"It looks to me to be in a very bad state of health," he said compassionately.

"It cost me twenty francs," she said, with some hesitation.

He seemed astonished. "Really! As much as that?"

"Yes, it was a capital article, and I wanted you to see the condition it is in."

"Yes, yes, I see; very well. But I really do not understand what it can have to do with me."

She began to feel uncomfortable; perhaps this company did not pay for such small articles, and she said:

"But—it is burned."

He could not deny it.

"I see that very well," he replied.

She remained open-mouthed, not knowing what to say next; then, suddenly recollecting that she had left out the main thing, she said hastily:

"I am Mme. Oreille; we are assured in La Maternelle, and I have come to claim the value of this damage."

"I only want you to have it re-covered," she added quickly, fearing a positive refusal.

The manager was rather embarrassed, and said: "But, really, madame, we do not sell umbrellas; we cannot undertake such kinds of repairs."

The little woman felt her courage reviving; she was not going to give up without a struggle; she was not even afraid any more, and said:

"I only want you to pay me the cost of repairing it; I can quite well get it done myself."

The gentleman seemed rather confused.

"Really, madame, it is such a very small matter! We are never asked to give compensation for such trivial losses. You must allow that we cannot make good pocket-handkerchiefs, gloves, brooms, slippers, all the small articles which are every day exposed to the chances of being burned."

She got red in the face, and felt inclined to fly into a rage.

"But, monsieur, last December one of our chimneys caught fire, and caused at least five hundred francs' damage; M. Oreille made no claim on the company, and so it is only just that it should pay for my umbrella now."

The manager, guessing that she was telling a lie, said, with a smile:

"You must acknowledge, madame, that it is very surprising that M. Oreille should have asked no compensation for damages amounting to five hundred francs, and should now claim five or six francs for mending an umbrella."

She was not the least put out, and replied:

"I beg your pardon, monsieur, the five hundred francs affected M. Oreille's pocket, whereas this damage, amounting to eighteen francs, concerns Mme. Oreille's pocket only, which is a totally different matter."

As he saw that he had no chance of getting rid of her, and that he would only be wasting his time, he said resignedly:

"Will you kindly tell me how the damage was done?"

She felt that she had won the victory, and said:

"This is how it happened, monsieur: In our hall there is a bronze stick and umbrella stand, and the other day, when I came in, I put my umbrella into it. I must tell you that just above there is a shelf for the candlesticks and matches. I put out my hand, took three or four matches, and struck one, but it missed fire, so I struck another, which ignited, but went out immediately, and a third did the same."

The manager interrupted her to make a joke.

"I suppose they were government matches, then?"

She did not understand him, and went on:

"Very likely. At any rate, the fourth caught fire, and I lit my candle, and went into my room to go to bed; but in a quarter of an hour I fancied that I smelt something burning, and I have always been terribly afraid of fire. If ever we have an accident it will not be my fault, I assure you. I am terribly nervous since our chimney was on fire, as I told you; so I got up, and hunted about everywhere, sniffing like a dog after game, and at last I noticed that my umbrella was burning. Most likely a match had fallen between the folds and burned it. You can see how it has damaged it."

The manager had taken his cue, and asked her: "What do you estimate the damage at?"

She did not know what to say, as she was not certain what value to put on it, but at last she replied:

"Perhaps you had better get it done yourself. I will leave it to you."

He, however, naturally refused.

"No, madame, I cannot do that. Tell me the amount of your

claim, that is all I want to know."

"Well, I think that—Look here, monsieur, I do not want to make any money out of you, so I will tell you what we will do. I will take my umbrella to the maker, who will re-cover it in good, durable silk, and I will bring the bill to you. Will that suit you, monsieur?"

"Perfectly, madame; we will settle it so. Here is a note for the cashier, who will repay you whatever it costs you."

He gave Mme. Oreille a slip of paper, who took it, got up and went out, thanking him, for she was in a hurry to escape lest he should change his mind.

She went briskly through the streets, looking out for a really good umbrella maker, and when she found a shop which appeared to be a first-class one, she went in, and said, confidently:

"I want this umbrella re-covered in silk, good silk. Use the very best and strongest you have; I don't mind what it costs."

BELHOMME'S BEAST

*T*he coach for Havre was ready to leave Criquetot, and all the passengers were waiting for their names to be called out, in the courtyard of the Commercial Hotel kept by Monsieur Malandain, Jr.

It was a yellow wagon, mounted on wheels which had once been yellow, but were now almost gray through the accumulation of mud. The front wheels were very small, the back ones, high and fragile, carried the large body of the vehicle, which was swollen like the belly of an animal. Three white horses, with enormous heads and great round knees, were the first things one noticed. They were harnessed ready to draw this coach, which had something of the appearance of a monster in its massive structure. The horses seemed already asleep in front of the strange vehicle.

The driver, Cesaire Horlaville, a little man with a big paunch, supple nevertheless, through his constant habit of climbing over the wheels to the top of the wagon, his face all aglow from exposure to the brisk air of the plains, to rain and storms, and also from the use of brandy, his eyes twitching from the effect of constant contact with wind and hail, appeared in the doorway of the hotel, wiping his mouth on the back of his hand. Large round baskets, full of frightened poultry, were standing in front of the peasant women. Cesaire Horlaville took them one after the other and packed them on the top of his coach; then more gently, he loaded on those containing eggs; finally he tossed up from below several little bags of grain, small packages wrapped in handkerchiefs, pieces of cloth, or paper. Then he opened the back door, and drawing a list from his pocket he called:

"Monsieur le cure de Gorgeville."

The priest advanced. He was a large, powerful, robust man with a red face and a genial expression. He hitched up his cassock to lift his foot, just as the women hold up their skirts, and climbed into the coach.

"The schoolmaster of Rollebose-les-Grinets."

The man hastened forward, tall, timid, wearing a long frock coat which fell to his knees, and he in turn disappeared through the open door.

"Maitre Poiret, two seats."

Poiret approached, a tall, round-shouldered man, bent by the plow, emaciated through abstinence, bony, with a skin dried by a sparing use of water. His wife followed him, small and thin, like a tired animal, carrying a large green umbrella in her hands.

"Maitre Rabot, two seats."

Rabot hesitated, being of an undecided nature. He asked: "You mean me?"

The driver was going to answer with a jest, when Rabot dived head first towards the door, pushed forward by a vigorous shove from his wife, a tall, square woman with a large, round stomach like a barrel, and hands as large as hams.

Rabot slipped into the wagon like a rat entering a hole.

"Maitre Caniveau."

A large peasant, heavier than an ox, made the springs bend, and was in turn engulfed in the interior of the yellow chest.

"Maitre Belhomme."

Belhomme, tall and thin, came forward, his neck bent, his head hanging, a handkerchief held to his ear as if he were suffering from a terrible toothache.

All these people wore the blue blouse over quaint and antique coats of a black or greenish cloth, Sunday clothes which they would only uncover in the streets of Havre. Their heads were covered by silk caps at high as towers, the emblem of supreme elegance in the small villages of Normandy.

Cesaire Horlaville closed the door, climbed up on his box and snapped his whip.

The three horses awoke and, tossing their heads, shook their bells.

The driver then yelling "Get up!" as loud as he could, whipped up his horses. They shook themselves, and, with an effort, started off at a slow, halting gait. And behind them came the coach, rattling its shaky windows and iron springs, making a terrible clatter of hardware and glass, while the passengers were tossed hither and thither like so many rubber balls.

At first all kept silent out of respect for the priest, that they might not shock him. Being of a loquacious and genial disposition, he started the conversation.

"Well, Maitre Caniveau," said he, "how are you getting along?"

The enormous farmer who, on account of his size, girth and stomach, felt a bond of sympathy for the representative of the Church, answered with a smile:

"Pretty well, Monsieur le cure, pretty well. And how are you?"

"Oh! I'm always well and healthy."

"And you, Maitre Poiret?" asked the abbe.

"Oh! I'd be all right only the colzas ain't a-goin' to give much this year, and times are so hard that they are the only things worth while raisin'."

"Well, what can you expect? Times are hard."

"Hub! I should say they were hard," sounded the rather virile voice of Rabot's big consort.

As she was from a neighboring village, the priest only knew her by name.

"Is that you, Blondel?" he said.

"Yes, I'm the one that married Rabot."

Rabot, slender, timid, and self-satisfied, bowed smilingly, bending his head forward as though to say: "Yes, I'm the Rabot whom Blondel married."

Suddenly Maitre Belhomme, still holding his handkerchief to his ear, began groaning in a pitiful fashion. He was going "Oh-oh-oh!" and stamping his foot in order to show his terrible suffering.

"You must have an awful toothache," said the priest.

The peasant stopped moaning for a minute and answered:

"No, Monsieur le cure, it is not the teeth. It's my ear-away down at the bottom of my ear."

"Well, what have you got in your ear? A lump of wax?"

"I don't know whether it's wax; but I know that it is a bug, a big bug, that crawled in while I was asleep in the haystack."

"A bug! Are you sure?"

"Am I sure? As sure as I am of heaven, Monsieur le cure! I can feel it gnawing at the bottom of my ear! It's eating my head for sure! It's eating my head! Oh-oh-oh!" And he began to stamp his foot again.

Great interest had been aroused among the spectators. Each one gave his bit of advice. Poiret claimed that it was a spider, the teacher, thought it might be a caterpillar. He had already seen such a thing once, at Campemuret, in Orne, where he had been for six years. In this case the caterpillar had gone through the head and out at the nose. But the man remained deaf in that ear ever after, the drum having been pierced.

"It's more likely to be a worm," said the priest.

Maitre Belhomme, his head resting against the door, for he had been the last one to enter, was still moaning.

"Oh—oh—oh! I think it must be an ant, a big ant—there it is biting again. Oh, Monsieur le cure, how it hurts! how it hurts!"

"Have you seen the doctor?" asked Caniveau.

"I should say not!"

"Why?"

The fear of the doctor seemed to cure Belhomme. He straightened up without, however, dropping his handkerchief.

"What! You have money for them, for those loafers? He would have come once, twice, three times, four times, five times! That means two five-franc pieces, two five-franc pieces, for sure. And what would he have done, the loafer, tell me, what would he have done? Can you tell me?"

Caniveau was laughing.

"No, I don't know. Where are you going?"

"I am going to Havre, to see Chambrelan."

"Who is Chambrelan?"

"The healer, of course."

"What healer?"

"The healer who cured my father."

"Your father?"

"Yes, the healer who cured my father years ago."

"What was the matter with your father?"

"A draught caught him in the back, so that he couldn't move hand or foot."

"Well, what did your friend Chambrelan do to him?"

"He kneaded his back with both hands as though he were making bread! And he was all right in a couple of hours!"

Belhomme thought that Chambrelan must also have used some charm, but he did not dare say so before the priest. Caniveau replied, laughing:

"Are you sure it isn't a rabbit that you have in your ear? He might have taken that hole for his home. Wait, I'll make him run away."

Whereupon Caniveau, making a megaphone of his hands, began to mimic the barking of hounds. He snapped, howled, growled, barked. And everybody in the carriage began to roar, even the schoolmaster, who, as a rule, never ever smiled.

However, as Belhomme seemed angry at their making fun of him, the priest changed the conversation and turning to Rabot's big wife, said:

"You have a large family, haven't you?"

"Oh, yes, Monsieur le cure—and it's a pretty hard matter to bring them up!"

Rabot agreed, nodding his head as though to say: "Oh, yes, it's a hard thing to bring up!"

"How many children?"

She replied authoritatively in a strong, clear voice:

"Sixteen children, Monsieur le cure, fifteen of them by my husband!"

And Rabot smiled broadly, nodding his head. He was responsible for fifteen, he alone, Rabot! His wife said so! Therefore there could be no doubt about it. And he was proud!

And whose was the sixteenth? She didn't tell. It was doubtless the first. Perhaps everybody knew, for no one was surprised. Even Caniveau kept mum.

But Belhomme began to moan again:

"Oh-oh-oh! It's scratching about in the bottom of my ear! Oh, dear, oh, dear!"

The coach just then stopped at the Cafe Polyto. The priest said:

"If someone were to pour a little water into your ear, it might perhaps drive it out. Do you want to try?"

"Sure! I am willing."

And everybody got out in order to witness the operation. The priest asked for a bowl, a napkin and a glass of water, then he told the teacher to hold the patient's head over on one side, and, as soon as the liquid should have entered the ear, to turn his head over suddenly on the other side.

But Caniveau, who was already peering into Belhomme's ear to see if he couldn't discover the beast, shouted:

"Gosh! What a mess! You'll have to clear that out, old man. Your rabbit could never get through that; his feet would stick."

The priest in turn examined the passage and saw that it was too narrow and too congested for him to attempt to expel the animal. It was the teacher who cleared out this passage by means of a match and a bit of cloth. Then, in the midst of the general excitement, the priest poured into the passage half a glass of water, which trickled over the face through the hair and down the neck of the patient. Then the schoolmaster quickly twisted the head round over the bowl, as though he were trying to unscrew it. A couple of drops dripped into the white bowl. All the passengers rushed forward. No insect had come out.

However, Belhomme exclaimed: "I don't feel anything any more." The priest triumphantly exclaimed: "Certainly it has been drowned." Everybody was happy and got back into the coach.

But hardly had they started when Belhomme began to cry out again. The bug had aroused itself and had become furious. He even declared that it had now entered his head and was eating his brain. He was howling with such contortions that Poiret's wife, thinking him possessed by the devil, began to cry and to cross herself. Then, the pain abating a little, the sick man began to tell how it was running round in his ear. With his finger he imitated the movements of the body, seeming to see it, to follow it with his eyes: "There it goes up again! Oh—oh—oh—what torture!"

Caniveau was getting impatient. "It's the water that is making the bug angry. It is probably more accustomed to wine."

Everybody laughed, and he continued: "When we get to the Cafe Bourbeux, give it some brandy, and it won't bother you any more, I wager."

But Belhomme could contain himself no longer; he began howling as though his soul were being torn from his body. The priest was obliged to hold his head for him. They asked Cesaire Horlaville to stop at the nearest house. It was a farmhouse at the side of the road. Belhomme was carried into it and laid on the kitchen table in order to repeat the operation. Caniveau advised mixing brandy and water in order to benumb and perhaps kill the insect. But the priest preferred vinegar.

They poured the liquid in drop by drop this time, that it might penetrate down to the bottom, and they left it several minutes in the organ that the beast had chosen for its home.

A bowl had once more been brought; Belhomme was turned over bodily by the priest and Caniveau, while the schoolmaster was tapping on the healthy ear in order to empty the other.

Cesaire Horlaville himself, whip in hand, had come in to observe the proceedings.

Suddenly, at the bottom of the bowl appeared a little brown spot, no bigger than a tiny seed. However, it was moving. It was a flea! First there were cries of astonishment and then shouts of laughter. A flea! Well, that was a good joke, a mighty good one! Caniveau was slapping his thigh, Cesaire Horlaville snapped his whip, the priest laughed like a braying donkey, the teacher cackled as though he were sneezing, and the two women were giving little screams of joy, like the clucking of hens.

Belhomme had seated himself on the table and had taken the bowl between his knees; he was observing, with serious attention and a vengeful anger in his eye, the conquered insect which was twisting round in the water. He grunted, "You rotten little beast!" and he spat on it.

The driver, wild with joy, kept repeating: "A flea, a flea, ah! there you are, damned little flea, damned little flea, damned little flea!" Then having calmed down a little, he cried: "Well, back to the coach! We've lost enough time."

DISCOVERY

The steamer was crowded with people and the crossing promised to be good. I was going from Havre to Trouville.

The ropes were thrown off, the whistle blew for the last time, the whole boat started to tremble, and the great wheels began to revolve, slowly at first, and then with ever-increasing rapidity.

We were gliding along the pier, black with people. Those on board were waving their handkerchiefs, as though they were leaving for America, and their friends on shore were answering in the same manner.

The big July sun was shining down on the red parasols, the light dresses, the joyous faces and on the ocean, barely stirred by a ripple. When we were out of the harbor, the little vessel swung round the big curve and pointed her nose toward the distant shore which was barely visible through the early morning mist. On our left was the broad estuary of the Seine, her muddy water, which never mingles with that of the ocean, making large yellow streaks clearly outlined against the immense sheet of the pure green sea.

As soon as I am on a boat I feel the need of walking to and fro, like a sailor on watch. Why? I do not know. Therefore I began to thread my way along the deck through the crowd of travellers. Suddenly I heard my name called. I turned around. I beheld one of my old friends, Henri Sidoine, whom I had not seen for ten years.

We shook hands and continued our walk together, talking of one thing or another. Suddenly Sidoine, who had been observing the crowd of passengers, cried out angrily:

"It's disgusting, the boat is full of English people!"

It was indeed full of them. The men were standing about, looking over the ocean with an all-important air, as though to say: "We are the English, the lords of the sea! Here we are!"

The young girls, formless, with shoes which reminded one of the naval constructions of their fatherland, wrapped in multi-colored shawls, were smiling vacantly at the magnificent scenery. Their small heads, planted at the top of their long bodies, wore English hats of the strangest build.

And the old maids, thinner yet, opening their characteristic jaws to the wind, seemed to threaten one with their long, yellow teeth. On passing them, one could notice the smell of rubber and of tooth wash.

Sidoine repeated, with growing anger:

"Disgusting! Can we never stop their coming to France?"

I asked, smiling:

"What have you got against them? As far as I am concerned, they don't worry me."

He snapped out:

"Of course they don't worry you! But I married one of them."

I stopped and laughed at him.

"Go ahead and tell me about it. Does she make you very unhappy?"

He shrugged his shoulders.

"No, not exactly."

"Then she—is not true to you?"

"Unfortunately, she is. That would be cause for a divorce, and I could get rid of her."

"Then I'm afraid I don't understand!"

"You don't understand? I'm not surprised. Well, she simply learned how to speak French—that's all! Listen.

"I didn't have the least desire of getting married when I went to spend the summer at Etretat two years ago. There is nothing more dangerous than watering-places. You have no idea how it suits young girls. Paris is the place for women and the country for young girls.

"Donkey rides, surf-bathing, breakfast on the grass, all these things are traps set for the marriageable man. And, really, there is nothing prettier than a child about eighteen, running through a field or picking flowers along the road.

"I made the acquaintance of an English family who were stopping at the same hotel where I was. The father looked like those men you see over there, and the mother was like all other Englishwomen.

"They had two sons, the kind of boys who play rough games with balls, bats or rackets from morning till night; then came two daughters, the elder a dry, shrivelled-up Englishwoman, the younger a dream of beauty, a heavenly blonde. When those chits make up their minds to be pretty, they are divine. This one had blue eyes, the kind of blue which seems to contain all the poetry, all the dreams, all the hopes and happiness of the world!

"What an infinity of dreams is caused by two such eyes! How well they answer the dim, eternal question of our heart!

"It must not be forgotten either that we Frenchmen adore foreign women. As soon as we meet a Russian, an Italian, a Swede, a Spaniard, or an Englishwoman with a pretty face, we immediately fall in love with her. We enthuse over everything which comes from outside—clothes, hats, gloves, guns and—women. But what a blunder!

"I believe that that which pleases us in foreign women is their accent. As soon as a woman speaks our language badly we think she is charming, if she uses the wrong word she is exquisite and if she jabbers in an entirely unintelligible jargon, she becomes irresistible.

"My little English girl, Kate, spoke a language to be marvelled at. At the beginning I could understand nothing, she invented so many new words; then I fell absolutely in love with this queer, amusing dialect. All maimed, strange, ridiculous terms became delightful in her mouth. Every evening, on the terrace of the Casino, we had long conversations which resembled spoken enigmas.

"I married her! I loved her wildly, as one can only love in a dream. For true lovers only love a dream which has taken the form of a woman.

"Well, my dear fellow, the most foolish thing I ever did was to give my wife a French teacher. As long as she slaughtered the dictionary and tortured the grammar I adored her. Our conversations were simple. They revealed to me her surprising gracefulness and matchless elegance; they showed her to me as a wonderful speaking jewel, a living doll made to be kissed, knowing, after a fashion, how to express what she loved. She reminded me of the pretty little toys which say 'papa' and 'mamma' when you pull a string.

"Now she talks—badly—very badly. She makes as many mistakes as ever—but I can understand her.

"I have opened my doll to look inside—and I have seen. And now I have to talk to her!

"Ah! you don't know, as I do, the opinions, the ideas, the theories of a well-educated young English girl, whom I can blame in nothing, and who repeats to me from morning till night sentences from a French reader prepared in England for the use of young ladies' schools.

"You have seen those cotillon favors, those pretty gilt papers, which enclose candies with an abominable taste. I have one of them. I tore it open. I wished to eat what was inside and it disgusted me so that I feel nauseated at seeing her compatriots.

"I have married a parrot to whom some old English governess might have taught French. Do you understand?"

The harbor of Trouville was now showing its wooden piers covered with people.

I said:

"Where is your wife?"

He answered:

"I took her back to Etretat."

"And you, where are you going?"

"I? Oh, I am going to rest up here at Trouville."

Then, after a pause, he added:

"You have no idea what a fool a woman can be at times!"

THE ACCURSED BREAD

*D*addy Taille had three daughters: Anna, the eldest, who was scarcely ever mentioned in the family; Rose, the second girl, who was eighteen, and Clara, the youngest, who was a girl of fifteen.

Old Taille was a widower and a foreman in M. Lebrument's button manufactory. He was a very upright man, very well thought of, abstemious; in fact, a sort of model workman. He lived at Havre, in the Rue d'Angouleme.

When Anna ran away from home the old man flew into a fearful rage. He threatened to kill the head clerk in a large draper's establishment in that town, whom he suspected. After a time, when he was told by various people that she was very steady and investing money in government securities, that she was no gadabout, but was a great friend of Monsieur Dubois, who was a judge of the Tribunal of Commerce, the father was appeased.

He even showed some anxiety as to how she was getting on, and asked some of her old friends who had been to see her, and when told that she had her own furniture, and that her mantelpiece was covered with vases and the walls with pictures, that there were clocks and carpets everywhere, he gave a broad contented smile. He had been working for thirty years to get together a wretched five or six thousand francs. This girl was evidently no fool.

One fine morning the son of Touchard, the cooper, at the other end of the street, came and asked him for the hand of Rose, the second girl. The old man's heart began to beat, for the Touchards were rich and in a good position. He was decidedly lucky with his girls.

The marriage was agreed upon, and it was settled that it should be a grand affair, and the wedding dinner was to be held at Sainte-Adresse, at Mother Jusa's restaurant. It would cost a lot certainly, but never mind, it did not matter just for once in a way.

But one morning, just as the old man was going home to luncheon with his two daughters, the door opened suddenly, and Anna appeared. She was well dressed and looked undeniably pretty and nice. She threw her arms round her father's neck before he could say a word, then fell into her sisters' arms with many tears and then asked for a plate, so that she might share the family soup. Taille was moved to tears in his turn and said several times:

"That is right, dear, that is right."

Then she told them about herself. She did not wish Rose's wedding to take place at Sainte-Adresse—certainly not. It should take place at her house and would cost her father nothing. She had settled everything and arranged everything, so it was "no good to say any more about it—there!"

"Very well, my dear! very well!" the old man said; "we will leave it so." But then he felt some doubt. Would the Touchards consent? But Rose, the bride-elect, was surprised and asked: "Why should they object, I should like to know? Just leave that to me; I will talk to Philip about it."

She mentioned it to her lover the very same day, and he declared it would suit him exactly. Father and Mother Touchard were naturally delighted at the idea of a good dinner which would cost them nothing and said:

"You may be quite sure that everything will be in first-rate style."

They asked to be allowed to bring a friend, Madame Florence, the cook on the first floor, and Anna agreed to everything.

The wedding was fixed for the last Tuesday of the month.

After the civil formalities and the religious ceremony the wedding party went to Anna's house. Among those whom the Tailles had brought was a cousin of a certain age, a Monsieur Sauvetanin, a man given to philosophical reflections, serious, and always very self-possessed, and Madame Lamondois, an old aunt.

Monsieur Sautevanin had been told off to give Anna his arm, as they were looked upon as the two most important persons in the company.

As soon as they had arrived at the door of Anna's house she let go her companion's arm, and ran on ahead, saying: "I will show you the way," and ran upstairs while the invited guests followed more slowly; and, when they got upstairs, she stood on one side to let them pass, and they rolled their eyes and turned their heads in all directions to admire this mysterious and luxurious dwelling.

The table was laid in the drawing-room, as the dining-room had been thought too small. Extra knives, forks and spoons had been hired from a neighboring restaurant, and decanters stood full of wine under the rays of the sun which shone in through the window.

The ladies went into the bedroom to take off their shawls and bonnets, and Father Touchard, who was standing at the door, made funny and suggestive signs to the men, with many a wink and nod. Daddy Taille, who thought a great deal of himself, looked with fatherly pride at his child's well-furnished rooms and went from one to the other, holding his hat in his hand, making a mental inventory of everything, and walking like a verger in a church.

Anna went backward and forward, ran about giving orders and hurrying on the wedding feast. Soon she appeared at the door of the dining-room and cried: "Come here, all of you, for a moment," and as the twelve guests entered the room they saw twelve glasses of Madeira on a small table.

Rose and her husband had their arms round each other's waists and were kissing each other in every corner. Monsieur Sauvetanin never took his eyes off Anna.

They sat down, and the wedding breakfast began, the relations sitting at one end of the table and the young people at the other. Madame Touchard, the mother, presided on the right and the bride on the left. Anna looked after everybody, saw that the glasses were kept filled and the plates well supplied. The guests evidently felt a certain respectful embarrassment at the sight of all the sumptuousness of the rooms and at the lavish manner in which they were treated. They all ate heartily of the good things provided, but there were no jokes such as are prevalent at weddings of that sort; it was all too grand, and it made them feel uncomfortable. Old Madame Touchard, who was fond of a bit of fun, tried to enliven matters a little, and at the beginning of the dessert she exclaimed: "I say, Philip, do sing us something." The neighbors in their street considered that he had the finest voice in all Havre.

The bridegroom got up, smiled, and, turning to his sister-in-law, from politeness and gallantry, tried to think of something suitable for the occasion, something serious and correct, to harmonize with the seriousness of the repast.

Anna had a satisfied look on her face, and leaned back in her chair to listen, and all assumed looks of attention, though prepared to smile should smiles be called for.

The singer announced "The Accursed Bread," and, extending his right arm, which made his coat ruck up into his neck, he began.

It was decidedly long, three verses of eight lines each, with the last line and the last but one repeated twice.

All went well for the first two verses; they were the usual commonplaces about bread gained by honest labor and by dishonesty. The aunt and the bride wept outright. The cook, who was present, at the end of the first verse looked at a roll which she held in her hand, with streaming eyes, as if it applied to her, while all applauded vigorously. At the end of the second verse the two servants, who were standing with their backs to the wall, joined loudly in the chorus, and the aunt and the bride wept outright.

Daddy Taille blew his nose with the noise of a trombone, and old Touchard brandished a whole loaf half over the table, and the cook shed silent tears on the crust which she was still holding.

Amid the general emotion Monsieur Sauvetanin said:

"That is the right sort of song; very different from the nasty, risky things one generally hears at weddings."

Anna, who was visibly affected, kissed her hand to her sister and pointed to her husband with an affectionate nod, as if to congratulate her.

Intoxicated by his success, the young man continued, and unfortunately the last verse contained words about the "bread of dishonor" gained by young girls who had been led astray. No one took up the refrain about this bread, supposed to be eaten with tears, except old Touchard and the two servants. Anna had grown deadly pale and cast down her eyes, while the bridegroom looked from one to the other without understanding the reason for this sudden coldness, and the cook hastily dropped the crust as if it were poisoned.

Monsieur Sauvetanin said solemnly, in order to save the situation: "That last couplet is not at all necessary"; and Daddy Taille, who had got red up to his ears, looked round the table fiercely.

Then Anna, her eyes swimming in tears, told the servants in the faltering voice of a woman trying to stifle her sobs, to bring the champagne.

All the guests were suddenly seized with exuberant joy, and all their faces became radiant again. And when old Touchard, who had seen, felt and understood nothing of what was going on, and pointing to the guests so as to emphasize his words, sang the last words of the refrain:

"Children, I warn you all to eat not of that bread," the whole company, when they saw the champagne bottles, with their necks covered with gold foil, appear, burst out singing, as if electrified by the sight:

"Children, I warn you all to eat not of that bread."

THE DOWRY

*T*he marriage of Maitre Simon Lebrument with Mademoiselle Jeanne Cordier was a surprise to no one. Maitre Lebrument had bought out the practice of Maitre Papillon; naturally, he had to have money to pay for it; and Mademoiselle Jeanne Cordier had three hundred thousand francs clear in currency, and in bonds payable to bearer.

Maitre Lebrument was a handsome man. He was stylish, although in a provincial way; but, nevertheless, he was stylish—a rare thing at Boutigny-le-Rebours.

Mademoiselle Cordier was graceful and fresh-looking, although a trifle awkward; nevertheless, she was a handsome girl, and one to be desired.

The marriage ceremony turned all Boutigny topsy-turvy. Everybody admired the young couple, who quickly returned home to domestic felicity, having decided simply to take a short trip to Paris, after a few days of retirement.

This tete-a-tete was delightful, Maitre Lebrument having shown just the proper amount of delicacy. He had taken as his motto: "Everything comes to him who waits." He knew how to be at the same time patient and energetic. His success was rapid and complete.

After four days, Madame Lebrument adored her husband. She could not get along without him. She would sit on his knees, and taking him by the ears she would say: "Open your mouth and shut your eyes." He would open his mouth wide and partly close his eyes, and he would try to nip her fingers as she slipped some dainty between his teeth. Then she would give him a kiss, sweet and long, which would make chills run up and down his spine. And then, in his turn, he would not have enough caresses to please his wife from morning to night and from night to morning.

When the first week was over, he said to his young companion:

"If you wish, we will leave for Paris next Tuesday. We will be like two lovers, we will go to the restaurants, the theatres, the concert halls, everywhere, everywhere!"

She was ready to dance for joy.

"Oh! yes, yes. Let us go as soon as possible."

He continued:

"And then, as we must forget nothing, ask your father to have your dowry ready; I shall pay Maitre Papillon on this trip."

She answered:

"All right: I will tell him to-morrow morning."

And he took her in his arms once more, to renew those sweet games of love which she had so enjoyed for the past week.

The following Tuesday, father-in-law and mother-in-law went to the station with their daughter and their son-in-law who were leaving for the capital.

The father-in-law said:

"I tell you it is very imprudent to carry so much money about in a pocketbook." And the young lawyer smiled.

"Don't worry; I am accustomed to such things. You understand that, in my profession, I sometimes have as much as a million about me. In this manner, at least we avoid a great amount of red tape and delay. You needn't worry."

The conductor was crying:

"All aboard for Paris!"

They scrambled into a car, where two old ladies were already seated.

Lebrument whispered into his wife's ear:

"What a bother! I won't be able to smoke."

She answered in a low voice

"It annoys me too, but not an account of your cigar."

The whistle blew and the train started. The trip lasted about an hour, during which time they did not say very much to each other, as the two old ladies did not go to sleep.

As soon as they were in front of the Saint-Lazare Station, Maitre Lebrument said to his wife:

"Dearie, let us first go over to the Boulevard and get something to eat; then we can quietly return and get our trunk and bring it to the hotel."

She immediately assented.

"Oh! yes. Let's eat at the restaurant. Is it far?"

He answered:

"Yes, it's quite a distance, but we will take the omnibus."

She was surprised:

"Why don't we take a cab?"

He began to scold her smilingly:

"Is that the way you save money? A cab for a five minutes' ride at six cents a minute! You would deprive yourself of nothing."

"That's so," she said, a little embarrassed.

A big omnibus was passing by, drawn by three big horses, which were trotting along. Lebrument called out:

"Conductor! Conductor!"

The heavy carriage stopped. And the young lawyer, pushing his wife, said to her quickly:

"Go inside; I'm going up on top, so that I may smoke at least one cigarette before lunch."

She had no time to answer. The conductor, who had seized her by the arm to help her up the step, pushed her inside, and she fell into a seat, bewildered, looking through the back window at the feet of her husband as he climbed up to the top of the vehicle.

And she sat there motionless, between a fat man who smelled of cheap tobacco and an old woman who smelled of garlic.

All the other passengers were lined up in silence—a grocer's boy, a young girl, a soldier, a gentleman with gold-rimmed spectacles and a big silk hat, two ladies with a self-satisfied and crabbed look, which seemed to say: "We are riding in this thing, but we don't have to," two sisters of charity and an undertaker. They looked like a collection of caricatures.

The jolting of the wagon made them wag their heads and the shaking of the wheels seemed to stupefy them—they all looked as though they were asleep.

The young woman remained motionless.

"Why didn't he come inside with me?" she was saying to herself. An unaccountable sadness seemed to be hanging over her. He really need not have acted so.

The sisters motioned to the conductor to stop, and they got off one after the other, leaving in their wake the pungent smell of camphor. The bus started tip and soon stopped again. And in got a cook, red-faced and out of breath. She sat down and placed her basket of provisions on her knees. A strong odor of dish-water filled the vehicle.

"It's further than I imagined," thought Jeanne.

The undertaker went out, and was replaced by a coachman who seemed to bring the atmosphere of the stable with him. The young girl had as a successor a messenger, the odor of whose feet showed that he was continually walking.

The lawyer's wife began to feel ill at ease, nauseated, ready to cry without knowing why.

Other persons left and others entered. The stage went on through interminable streets, stopping at stations and starting again.

"How far it is!" thought Jeanne. "I hope he hasn't gone to sleep!

He has been so tired the last few days."

Little by little all the passengers left. She was left alone, all alone. The conductor cried:

"Vaugirard!"

Seeing that she did not move, he repeated:

"Vaugirard!"

She looked at him, understanding that he was speaking to her, as there was no one else there. For the third time the man said:

"Vaugirard!"

Then she asked:

"Where are we?"

He answered gruffly:

"We're at Vaugirard, of course! I have been yelling it for the last half hour!"

"Is it far from the Boulevard?" she said.

"Which boulevard?"

"The Boulevard des Italiens."

"We passed that a long time ago!"

"Would you mind telling my husband?"

"Your husband! Where is he?"

"On the top of the bus."

"On the top! There hasn't been anybody there for a long time."

She started, terrified.

"What? That's impossible! He got on with me. Look well! He must be there."

The conductor was becoming uncivil:

"Come on, little one, you've talked enough! You can find ten men for every one that you lose. Now run along. You'll find another one somewhere."

Tears were coming to her eyes. She insisted:

"But, monsieur, you are mistaken; I assure you that you must be mistaken. He had a big portfolio under his arm."

The man began to laugh:

"A big portfolio! Oh, yes! He got off at the Madeleine. He got rid of you, all right! Ha! ha! ha!"

The stage had stopped. She got out and, in spite of herself, she looked up instinctively to the roof of the bus. It was absolutely deserted.

Then she began to cry, and, without thinking that anybody was listening or watching her, she said out loud:

"What is going to become of me?"

An inspector approached:

"What's the matter?"

The conductor answered, in a bantering tone of voice:

"It's a lady who got left by her husband during the trip."

The other continued:

"Oh! that's nothing. You go about your business."

Then he turned on his heels and walked away.

She began to walk straight ahead, too bewildered, too crazed even to understand what had happened to her. Where was she to go? What could she do? What could have happened to him? How could he have made such a mistake? How could he have been so forgetful?

She had two francs in her pocket. To whom could she go? Suddenly she remembered her cousin Barral, one of the assistants in the offices of the Ministry of the Navy.

She had just enough to pay for a cab. She drove to his house. He met her just as he was leaving for his office. He was carrying a large portfolio under his arm, just like Lebrument.

She jumped out of the carriage.

"Henry!" she cried.

He stopped, astonished:

"Jeanne! Here—all alone! What are you doing? Where have you come from?"

Her eyes full of tears, she stammered:

"My husband has just got lost!"

"Lost! Where?"

"On an omnibus."

"On an omnibus?"

Weeping, she told him her whole adventure.

He listened, thought, and then asked:

"Was his mind clear this morning?"

"Yes."

"Good. Did he have much money with him?"

"Yes, he was carrying my dowry."

"Your dowry! The whole of it?"

"The whole of it—in order to pay for the practice which he bought."

"Well, my dear cousin, by this time your husband must be well on his way to Belgium."

She could not understand. She kept repeating:

"My husband—you say—"

"I say that he has disappeared with your—your capital—that's all!"

She stood there, a prey to conflicting emotions, sobbing.

"Then he is—he is—he is a villain!"

And, faint from excitement, she leaned her head on her cousin's shoulder and wept.

As people were stopping to look at them, he pushed her gently into the vestibule of his house, and, supporting her with his arm around her waist, he led her up the stairs, and as his astonished servant opened the door, he ordered:

"Sophie, run to the restaurant and get a luncheon for two. I am not going to the office to-day."

THE DIARY OF A MADMAN

*H*e was dead—the head of a high tribunal, the upright magistrate whose irreproachable life was a proverb in all the courts of France. Advocates, young counsellors, judges had greeted him at sight of his large, thin, pale face lighted up by two sparkling deep-set eyes, bowing low in token of respect.

He had passed his life in pursuing crime and in protecting the weak. Swindlers and murderers had no more redoubtable enemy, for he seemed to read the most secret thoughts of their minds.

He was dead, now, at the age of eighty-two, honored by the homage and followed by the regrets of a whole people. Soldiers in red trousers had escorted him to the tomb and men in white cravats had spoken words and shed tears that seemed to be sincere beside his grave.

But here is the strange paper found by the dismayed notary in the desk where he had kept the records of great criminals! It was entitled: WHY?

20th June, 1851. I have just left court. I have condemned Blondel to death! Now, why did this man kill his five children? Frequently one meets with people to whom the destruction of life is a pleasure. Yes, yes, it should be a pleasure, the greatest of all, perhaps, for is not killing the next thing to creating? To make and to destroy! These two words contain the history of the universe, all the history of worlds, all that is, all! Why is it not intoxicating to kill?

25th June. To think that a being is there who lives, who walks, who runs. A being? What is a being? That animated thing, that bears in it the principle of motion and a will ruling that motion. It is attached to nothing, this thing. Its feet do not belong to the ground. It is a grain of life that moves on the earth, and this grain of life, coming I know not whence, one can destroy at one's will. Then nothing—nothing more. It perishes, it is finished.

26th June. Why then is it a crime to kill? Yes, why? On the contrary, it is the law of nature. The mission of every being is to kill; he kills to live, and he kills to kill. The beast kills without ceasing, all day, every instant of his existence. Man kills without ceasing, to nourish himself; but since he needs, besides, to kill for pleasure, he has invented hunting! The child kills the insects he finds, the little birds, all the little animals that come in his way. But this does not suffice for the irresistible need to massacre that is in us. It is not enough to kill beasts; we must kill man too. Long ago this need was satisfied by human sacrifices. Now the requirements of social life have made murder a crime. We condemn and punish the assassin! But as we cannot live without yielding to this natural and imperious instinct of death, we relieve ourselves, from time to time, by wars. Then a whole nation slaughters another nation. It is a feast of blood, a feast that maddens armies and that intoxicates civilians, women and children, who read, by lamplight at night, the feverish story of massacre.

One might suppose that those destined to accomplish these butcheries of men would be despised! No, they are loaded with honors. They are clad in gold and in resplendent garments; they wear plumes on their heads and ornaments on their breasts, and they are given crosses, rewards, titles of every kind. They are proud, respected, loved by women, cheered by the crowd, solely because their mission is to shed human blood; They drag through the streets their instruments of death, that the passer-by, clad in black, looks on with envy. For to kill is the great law set by nature in the heart of existence! There is nothing more beautiful and honorable than killing!

30th June. To kill is the law, because nature loves eternal youth. She seems to cry in all her unconscious acts: "Quick! quick! quick!" The more she destroys, the more she renews herself.

2d July. A human being—what is a human being? Through thought it is a reflection of all that is; through memory and science it is an abridged edition of the universe whose history it represents, a mirror of things and of nations, each human being becomes a microcosm in the macrocosm.

3d July. It must be a pleasure, unique and full of zest, to kill; to have there before one the living, thinking being; to make therein a little hole, nothing but a little hole, to see that red thing flow which is the blood, which makes life; and to have before one only a heap of limp flesh, cold, inert, void of thought!

5th August. I, who have passed my life in judging, condemning, killing by the spoken word, killing by the guillotine those who had killed by the knife, I, I, if I should do as all the assassins have done whom I have smitten, I—I—who would know it?

10th August. Who would ever know? Who would ever suspect me, me, me, especially if I should choose a being I had no interest in doing away with?

15th August. The temptation has come to me. It pervades my whole being; my hands tremble with the desire to kill.

22d August. I could resist no longer. I killed a little creature as an experiment, for a beginning. Jean, my servant, had a goldfinch in a cage hung in the office window. I sent him on an errand, and I took the little bird in my hand, in my hand where I felt its heart beat. It was warm. I went up to my room. From time to time I squeezed it tighter; its heart beat faster; this was atrocious and delicious. I was near choking it. But I could not see the blood.

Then I took scissors, short-nail scissors, and I cut its throat with three slits, quite gently. It opened its bill, it struggled to escape me, but I held it, oh! I held it—I could have held a mad dog—and I saw the blood trickle.

And then I did as assassins do—real ones. I washed the scissors, I washed my hands. I sprinkled water and took the body, the corpse, to the garden to hide it. I buried it under a strawberry-plant. It will never be found. Every day I shall eat a strawberry from that plant. How one can enjoy life when one knows how!

My servant cried; he thought his bird flown. How could he suspect me? Ah! ah!

25th August. I must kill a man! I must—

30th August. It is done. But what a little thing! I had gone for a walk in the forest of Vernes. I was thinking of nothing, literally nothing. A child was in the road, a little child eating a slice of bread and butter.

He stops to see me pass and says, "Good-day, Mr. President."

And the thought enters my head, "Shall I kill him?"

I answer: "You are alone, my boy?"

"Yes, sir."

"All alone in the wood?"

"Yes, sir."

The wish to kill him intoxicated me like wine. I approached him quite softly, persuaded that he was going to run away. And, suddenly, I seized him by the throat. He looked at me with terror in his eyes—such eyes! He held my wrists in his little hands and his body writhed like a feather over the fire. Then he moved no more. I threw the body in the ditch, and some weeds on top of it. I returned home, and dined well. What a little thing it was! In the evening I was very gay, light, rejuvenated; I passed the evening at the Prefect's. They found me witty. But I have not seen blood! I am tranquil.

31st August. The body has been discovered. They are hunting

for the assassin. Ah! ah!

1st September. Two tramps have been arrested. Proofs are lacking.

2d September. The parents have been to see me. They wept! Ah! ah!

6th October. Nothing has been discovered. Some strolling vagabond must have done the deed. Ah! ah! If I had seen the blood flow, it seems to me I should be tranquil now! The desire to kill is in my blood; it is like the passion of youth at twenty.

20th October. Yet another. I was walking by the river, after breakfast. And I saw, under a willow, a fisherman asleep. It was noon. A spade was standing in a potato-field near by, as if expressly, for me.

I took it. I returned; I raised it like a club, and with one blow of the edge I cleft the fisherman's head. Oh! he bled, this one! Rose-colored blood. It flowed into the water, quite gently. And I went away with a grave step. If I had been seen! Ah! ah! I should have made an excellent assassin.

25th October. The affair of the fisherman makes a great stir. His nephew, who fished with him, is charged with the murder.

26th October. The examining magistrate affirms that the nephew is guilty. Everybody in town believes it. Ah! ah!

27th October. The nephew makes a very poor witness. He had gone to the village to buy bread and cheese, he declared. He swore that his uncle had been killed in his absence! Who would believe him?

28th October. The nephew has all but confessed, they have badgered him so. Ah! ah! justice!

15th November. There are overwhelming proofs against the nephew, who was his uncle's heir. I shall preside at the sessions.

25th January. To death! to death! to death! I have had him condemned to death! Ah! ah! The advocate-general spoke like an angel! Ah! ah! Yet another! I shall go to see him executed!

10th March. It is done. They guillotined him this morning. He died very well! very well! That gave me pleasure! How fine it is to see a man's head cut off!

Now, I shall wait, I can wait. It would take such a little thing to let myself be caught.

The manuscript contained yet other pages, but without relating any new crime.

Alienist physicians to whom the awful story has been submitted declare that there are in the world many undiscovered madmen as adroit and as much to be feared as this monstrous lunatic.

THE MASK

There was a masquerade ball at the Elysee-Montmartre that evening. It was the 'Mi-Careme', and the crowds were pouring into the brightly lighted passage which leads to the dance ball, like water flowing through the open lock of a canal. The loud call of the orchestra, bursting like a storm of sound, shook the rafters, swelled through the whole neighborhood and awoke, in the streets and in the depths of the houses, an irresistible desire to jump, to get warm, to have fun, which slumbers within each human animal.

The patrons came from every quarter of Paris; there were people of all classes who love noisy pleasures, a little low and tinged with debauch. There were clerks and girls—girls of every description, some wearing common cotton, some the finest batiste; rich girls, old and covered with diamonds, and poor girls of sixteen, full of the desire to revel, to belong to men, to spend money. Elegant black evening suits, in search of fresh or faded but appetizing novelty, wandering through the excited crowds, looking, searching, while the masqueraders seemed moved above all by the desire for amusement. Already the far-famed quadrilles had attracted around them a curious crowd. The moving hedge which encircled the four dancers swayed in and out like a snake, sometimes nearer and sometimes farther away, according to the motions of the performers. The two women, whose lower limbs seemed to be attached to their bodies by rubber springs, were making wonderful and surprising motions with their legs. Their partners hopped and skipped about, waving their arms about. One could imagine their panting breath beneath their masks.

One of them, who had taken his place in the most famous quadrille, as substitute for an absent celebrity, the handsome "Songe-au-Gosse," was trying to keep up with the tireless "Arete-de-Veau" and was making strange fancy steps which aroused the joy and sarcasm of the audience.

He was thin, dressed like a dandy, with a pretty varnished mask on his face. It had a curly blond mustache and a wavy wig. He looked like a wax figure from the Musee Grevin, like a strange and fantastic caricature of the charming young man of fashion plates, and he danced with visible effort, clumsily, with a comical impetuosity. He appeared rusty beside the others when he tried to imitate their gambols: he seemed overcome by rheumatism, as heavy as a great Dane playing with greyhounds. Mocking bravos encouraged him. And he, carried away with enthusiasm, jigged about with such frenzy that suddenly, carried away by a wild spurt, he pitched head foremost into the living wall formed by the audience, which opened up before him to allow him to pass, then closed around the inanimate body of the dancer, stretched out on his face.

Some men picked him up and carried him away, calling for a doctor. A gentleman stepped forward, young and elegant, in well-fitting evening clothes, with large pearl studs. "I am a professor of the Faculty of Medicine," he said in a modest voice. He was allowed to pass, and he entered a small room full of little cardboard boxes, where the still lifeless dancer had been stretched out on some chairs. The doctor at first wished to take off the mask, and he noticed that it was attached in a complicated manner, with a perfect network of small metal wires which cleverly bound it to his wig and covered the whole head. Even the neck was imprisoned in a false skin which continued the chin and was painted the color of flesh, being attached to the collar of the shirt.

All this had to be cut with strong scissors. When the physician had slit open this surprising arrangement, from the shoulder to the temple, he opened this armor and found the face of an old man, worn out, thin and wrinkled. The surprise among those who had brought in this seemingly young dancer was so great that no one laughed, no one said a word.

All were watching this sad face as he lay on the straw chairs, his eyes closed, his face covered with white hair, some long, falling from the forehead over the face, others short, growing around the face and the chin, and beside this poor head, that pretty little, neat varnished, smiling mask.

The man regained consciousness after being inanimate for a long time, but he still seemed to be so weak and sick that the physician feared some dangerous complication. He asked: "Where do you live?"

The old dancer seemed to be making an effort to remember, and then he mentioned the name of the street, which no one knew. He was asked for more definite information about the neighborhood. He answered with a great slowness, indecision and difficulty, which revealed his upset state of mind. The physician continued:

"I will take you home myself."

Curiosity had overcome him to find out who this strange dancer, this phenomenal jumper might be. Soon the two rolled away in a cab to the other side of Montmartre.

They stopped before a high building of poor appearance. They went up a winding staircase. The doctor held to the banister, which was so grimy that the hand stuck to it, and he supported the dizzy old man, whose forces were beginning to return. They stopped at the fourth floor.

The door at which they had knocked was opened by an old woman, neat looking, with a white nightcap enclosing a thin face with sharp features, one of those good, rough faces of a hard-working and faithful woman. She cried out:

"For goodness sake! What's the matter?"

He told her the whole affair in a few words. She became reassured and even calmed the physician himself by telling him that the same thing had happened many times. She said: "He must be put to bed, monsieur, that is all. Let him sleep and tomorrow he will be all right."

The doctor continued: "But he can hardly speak."

"Oh! that's just a little drink, nothing more; he has eaten no dinner, in order to be nimble, and then he took a few absinthes in order to work himself up to the proper pitch. You see, drink gives strength to his legs, but it stops his thoughts and words. He is too old to dance as he does. Really, his lack of common sense is enough to drive one mad!"

The doctor, surprised, insisted:

"But why does he dance like that at his age?"

She shrugged her shoulders and turned red from the anger which was slowly rising within her and she cried out:

"Ah! yes, why? So that the people will think him young under his mask; so that the women will still take him for a young dandy and whisper nasty things into his ears; so that he can rub up against all their dirty skins, with their perfumes and powders and cosmetics. Ah! it's a fine business! What a life I have had for the last forty years! But we must first get him to bed, so that he may have no ill effects. Would you mind helping me? When he is like that I can't do anything with him alone."

The old man was sitting on his bed, with a tipsy look, his long white hair falling over his face. His companion looked at him with tender yet indignant eyes. She continued:

"Just see the fine head he has for his age, and yet he has to go and disguise himself in order to make people think that he is young. It's a perfect shame! Really, he has a fine head, monsieur! Wait, I'll show it to you before putting him to bed."

She went to a table on which stood the washbasin a pitcher of water, soap and a comb and brush. She took the brush, returned to the bed and pushed back the drunkard's tangled hair. In a few seconds she made him look like a model fit for a great painter, with his long white locks flowing on his neck. Then she stepped back in order to observe him, saying: "There! Isn't he fine for his age?"

"Very," agreed the doctor, who was beginning to be highly amused.

She added: "And if you had known him when he was twenty-five! But we must get him to bed, otherwise the drink will make him sick. Do you mind drawing off that sleeve? Higher-like that-that's right. Now the trousers. Wait, I will take his shoes off—that's right. Now, hold him upright while I open the bed. There—let us put him in. If you think that he is going to disturb himself when it is time for me to get in you are mistaken. I have to find a little corner any place I can. That doesn't bother him! Bah! You old pleasure seeker!"

As soon as he felt himself stretched out in his sheets the old man closed his eyes, opened them closed them again, and over his whole face appeared an energetic resolve to sleep. The doctor examined him with an ever-increasing interest and asked: "Does he go to all the fancy balls and try to be a young man?" "To all of them, monsieur, and he comes back to me in the morning in a deplorable condition. You see, it's regret that leads him on and that makes him put a pasteboard face over his own. Yes, the regret of no longer being what he was and of no longer making any conquests!"

He was sleeping now and beginning to snore. She looked at him with a pitying expression and continued: "Oh! how many conquests that man has made! More than one could believe, monsieur, more than the finest gentlemen of the world, than all the tenors and all the generals."

"Really? What did he do?"

"Oh! it will surprise you at first, as you did not know him in his palmy days. When I met him it was also at a ball, for he has always frequented them. As soon as I saw him I was caught—caught like a fish on a hook. Ah! how pretty he was, monsieur, with his curly raven locks and black eyes as large as saucers! Indeed, he was good looking! He took me away that evening and

I never have left him since, never, not even for a day, no matter what he did to me! Oh! he has often made it hard for me!"

The doctor asked: "Are you married?"

She answered simply: "Yes, monsieur, otherwise he would have dropped me as he did the others. I have been his wife and his servant, everything, everything that he wished. How he has made me cry—tears which I did not show him; for he would tell all his adventures to me—to me, monsieur—without understanding how it hurt me to listen."

"But what was his business?"

"That's so. I forgot to tell you. He was the foreman at Martel's—a foreman such as they never had had—an artist who averaged ten francs an hour."

"Martel?—who is Martel?"

"The hairdresser, monsieur, the great hairdresser of the Opera, who had all the actresses for customers. Yes, sir, all the smartest actresses had their hair dressed by Ambrose and they would give him tips that made a fortune for him. Ah! monsieur, all the women are alike, yes, all of them. When a man pleases their fancy they offer themselves to him. It is so easy—and it hurt me so to hear about it. For he would tell me everything—he simply could not hold his tongue—it was impossible. Those things please the men so much! They seem to get even more enjoyment out of telling than doing.

"When I would see him coming in the evening, a little pale, with a pleased look and a bright eye, would say to myself: 'One more. I am sure that he has caught one more.' Then I felt a wild desire to question him and then, again, not to know, to stop his talking if he should begin. And we would look at each other.

"I knew that he would not keep still, that he would come to the point. I could feel that from his manner, which seemed to laugh and say: 'I had a fine adventure to-day, Madeleine.' I would pretend to notice nothing, to guess nothing; I would set the table, bring on the soup and sit down opposite him.

"At those times, monsieur, it was as if my friendship for him had been crushed in my body as with a stone. It hurt. But he did not understand; he did not know; he felt a need to tell all those things to some one, to boast, to show how much he was loved, and I was the only one he had to whom he could talk-the only one. And I would have to listen and drink it in, like poison.

"He would begin to take his soup and then he would say: 'One more, Madeleine.'

"And I would think: 'Here it comes! Goodness! what a man!

Why did I ever meet him?'

"Then he would begin: 'One more! And a beauty, too.' And it would be some little one from the Vaudeville or else from the Varietes, and some of the big ones, too, some of the most famous. He would tell me their names, how their apartments were furnished, everything, everything, monsieur. Heartbreaking details. And he would go over them and tell his story over again from beginning to end, so pleased with himself that I would pretend to laugh so that he would not get angry with me.

"Everything may not have been true! He liked to glorify himself and was quite capable of inventing such things! They may perhaps also have been true! On those evenings he would pretend to be tired and wish to go to bed after supper. We would take supper at eleven, monsieur, for he could never get back from work earlier.

"When he had finished telling about his adventure he would walk round the room and smoke cigarettes, and he was so handsome, with his mustache and curly hair, that I would think: 'It's true, just the same, what he is telling. Since I myself am crazy about that man, why should not others be the same?' Then I would feel like crying, shrieking, running away and jumping out of the window while I was clearing the table and he was smoking. He would yawn in order to show how tired he was, and he would say two or three times before going to bed: 'Ah! how well I shall sleep this evening!'

"I bear him no ill will, because he did not know how he was hurting me. No, he could not know! He loved to boast about the women just as a peacock loves to show his feathers. He got to the point where he thought that all of them looked at him and desired him.

"It was hard when he grew old. Oh, monsieur, when I saw his first white hair I felt a terrible shock and then a great joy—a wicked joy—but so great, so great! I said to myself: 'It's the end-it's the end.' It seemed as if I were about to be released from prison. At last I could have him to myself, all to myself, when the others would no longer want him.

"It was one morning in bed. He was still sleeping and I leaned over him to wake him up with a kiss, when I noticed in his curls, over his temple, a little thread which shone like silver. What a surprise! I should not have thought it possible! At first I thought of tearing it out so that he would not see it, but as I looked carefully I noticed another farther up. White hair! He was going to have white hair! My heart began to thump and perspiration stood out all over me, but away down at the bottom I was happy.

"It was mean to feel thus, but I did my housework with a light heart that morning, without waking him up, and, as soon as he opened his eyes of his own accord, I said to him: 'Do you know what I discovered while you were asleep?'

"'No.'

"'I found white hairs.'

"He started up as if I had tickled him and said angrily: 'It's not true!'

"'Yes, it is. There are four of them over your left temple.'

"He jumped out of bed and ran over to the mirror. He could not find them. Then I showed him the first one, the lowest, the little curly one, and I said: 'It's no wonder, after the life that you have been leading. In two years all will be over for you.'

"Well, monsieur, I had spoken true; two years later one could not recognize him. How quickly a man changes! He was still handsome, but he had lost his freshness, and the women no longer ran after him. Ah! what a life I led at that time! How he treated me! Nothing suited him. He left his trade to go into the hat business, in which he ate up all his money. Then he unsuccessfully tried to be an actor, and finally he began to frequent public balls. Fortunately, he had had common sense enough to save a little something on which we now live. It is sufficient, but it is not enormous. And to think that at one time he had almost a fortune.

"Now you see what he does. This habit holds him like a frenzy. He has to be young; he has to dance with women who smell of perfume and cosmetics. You poor old darling!"

She was looking at her old snoring husband fondly, ready to cry. Then, gently tiptoeing up to him, she kissed his hair. The physician had risen and was getting ready to leave, finding nothing to say to this strange couple. Just as he was leaving she asked:

"Would you mind giving me your address? If he should grow worse, I could go and get you."

THE PENGUINS' ROCK

This is the season for penguins.

From April to the end of May, before the Parisian visitors arrive, one sees, all at once, on the little beach at Etretat several old gentlemen, booted and belted in shooting costume. They spend four or five days at the Hotel Hauville, disappear, and return again three weeks later. Then, after a fresh sojourn, they go away altogether.

One sees them again the following spring.

These are the last penguin hunters, what remain of the old set. There were about twenty enthusiasts thirty or forty years ago; now there are only a few of the enthusiastic sportsmen.

The penguin is a very rare bird of passage, with peculiar habits. It lives the greater part of the year in the latitude of Newfoundland and the islands of St. Pierre and Miquelon. But in the breeding season a flight of emigrants crosses the ocean and comes every year to the same spot to lay their eggs, to the Penguins' Rock near Etretat. They are found nowhere else, only there. They have always come there, have always been chased away, but return again, and will always return. As soon as the young birds are grown they all fly away, and disappear for a year.

Why do they not go elsewhere? Why not choose some other spot on the long white, unending cliff that extends from the Pas-de-Calais to Havre? What force, what invincible instinct, what custom of centuries impels these birds to come back to this place? What first migration, what tempest, possibly, once cast their ancestors on this rock? And why do the children, the grandchildren, all the descendants of the first parents always return here?

There are not many of them, a hundred at most, as if one single family, maintaining the tradition, made this annual pilgrimage.

And each spring, as soon as the little wandering tribe has taken up its abode an the rock, the same sportsmen also reappear in the village. One knew them formerly when they were young; now they are old, but constant to the regular appointment which they have kept for thirty or forty years. They would not miss it for anything in the world.

It was an April evening in one of the later years. Three of the old sportsmen had arrived; one was missing—M. d'Arnelles.

He had written to no one, given no account of himself. But he was not dead, like so many of the rest; they would have heard of it. At length, tired of waiting for him, the other three sat down to table. Dinner was almost over when a carriage drove into the yard of the hotel, and the late corner presently entered the dining room.

He sat down, in a good humor, rubbing his hands, and ate with zest. When one of his comrades remarked with surprise at his being in a frock-coat, he replied quietly:

"Yes, I had no time to change my clothes."

They retired on leaving the table, for they had to set out before daybreak in order to take the birds unawares.

There is nothing so pretty as this sport, this early morning expedition.

At three o'clock in the morning the sailors awoke the sportsmen by throwing sand against the windows. They were ready in a few minutes and went down to the beach. Although it was still dark, the stars had paled a little. The sea ground the shingle on the beach. There was such a fresh breeze that it made one shiver slightly in spite of one's heavy clothing.

Presently two boats were pushed down the beach, by the sailors, with a sound as of tearing cloth, and were floated on the nearest waves. The brown sail was hoisted, swelled a little, fluttered, hesitated and swelling out again as round as a paunch, carried the boats towards the large arched entrance that could be faintly distinguished in the darkness.

The sky became clearer, the shadows seemed to melt away. The coast still seemed veiled, the great white coast, perpendicular as a wall.

They passed through the Manne-Porte, an enormous arch beneath which a ship could sail; they doubled the promontory of La Courtine, passed the little valley of Antifer and the cape of the same name; and suddenly caught sight of a beach on which some hundreds of seagulls were perched.

That was the Penguins' Rock. It was just a little protuberance of the cliff, and on the narrow ledges of rock the birds' heads might be seen watching the boats.

They remained there, motionless, not venturing to fly off as yet. Some of them perched on the edges, seated upright, looked almost like bottles, for their little legs are so short that when they walk they glide along as if they were on rollers. When they start to fly they cannot make a spring and let themselves fall like stones almost down to the very men who are watching them.

They know their limitation and the danger to which it subjects them, and cannot make up their minds to fly away.

But the boatmen begin to shout, beating the sides of the boat with the wooden boat pins, and the birds, in affright, fly one by one into space until they reach the level of the waves. Then, moving their wings rapidly, they scud, scud along until they reach the open sea; if a shower of lead does not knock them into the water.

For an hour the firing is kept up, obliging them to give up, one after another. Sometimes the mother birds will not leave their nests, and are riddled with shot, causing drops of blood to spurt out on the white cliff, and the animal dies without having deserted her eggs.

The first day M. d'Arnelles fired at the birds with his habitual zeal; but when the party returned toward ten o'clock, beneath a brilliant sun, which cast great triangles of light on the white cliffs along the coast he appeared a little worried, and absentminded, contrary to his accustomed manner.

As soon as they got on shore a kind of servant dressed in black came up to him and said something in a low tone. He seemed to reflect, hesitate, and then replied:

"No, to-morrow."

The following day they set out again. This time M, d'Arnelles frequently missed his aim, although the birds were close by. His friends teased him, asked him if he were in love, if some secret sorrow was troubling his mind and heart. At length he confessed.

"Yes, indeed, I have to leave soon, and that annoys me."

"What, you must leave? And why?"

"Oh, I have some business that calls me back. I cannot stay any longer."

They then talked of other matters.

As soon as breakfast was over the valet in black appeared. M. d'Arnelles ordered his carriage, and the man was leaving the room when the three sportsmen interfered, insisting, begging, and praying their friend to stay. One of them at last said:

"Come now, this cannot be a matter of such importance, for you have already waited two days."

M. d'Arnelles, altogether perplexed, began to think, evidently baffled, divided between pleasure and duty, unhappy and disturbed.

After reflecting for some time he stammered:

"The fact is—the fact is—I am not alone here. I have my son-in-law."

There were exclamations and shouts of "Your son-in-law! Where is he?"

He suddenly appeared confused and his face grew red.

"What! do you not know? Why—why—he is in the coach house. He is dead."

They were all silent in amazement.

M. d'Arnelles continued, more and more disturbed:

"I had the misfortune to lose him; and as I was taking the body to my house, in Briseville, I came round this way so as not to miss our appointment. But you can see that I cannot wait any longer."

Then one of the sportsmen, bolder than the rest said:

"Well, but—since he is dead—it seems to me that he can wait a day longer."

The others chimed in:

"That cannot be denied."

M. d'Arnelles appeared to be relieved of a great weight, but a little uneasy, nevertheless, he asked:

"But, frankly—do you think—"

The three others, as one man, replied:

"Parbleu! my dear boy, two days more or less can make no difference in his present condition."

And, perfectly calmly, the father-in-law turned to the undertaker's assistant, and said:

"Well, then, my friend, it will be the day after tomorrow."

A FAMILY

I was to see my old friend, Simon Radevin, of whom I had lost sight for fifteen years. At one time he was my most intimate friend, the friend who knows one's thoughts, with whom one passes long, quiet, happy evenings, to whom one tells one's secret love affairs, and who seems to draw out those rare, ingenious, delicate thoughts born of that sympathy that gives a sense of repose.

For years we had scarcely been separated; we had lived, travelled, thought and dreamed together; had liked the same things, had admired the same books, understood the same authors, trembled with the same sensations, and very often laughed at the same individuals, whom we understood completely by merely exchanging a glance.

Then he married. He married, quite suddenly, a little girl from the provinces, who had come to Paris in search of a husband. How in the world could that little thin, insipidly fair girl, with her weak hands, her light, vacant eyes, and her clear, silly voice, who was exactly like a hundred thousand marriageable dolls, have picked up that intelligent, clever young fellow? Can any one understand these things? No doubt he had hoped for happiness, simple, quiet and long-enduring happiness, in the arms of a good, tender and faithful woman; he had seen all that in the transparent looks of that schoolgirl with light hair.

He had not dreamed of the fact that an active, living and vibrating man grows weary of everything as soon as he understands the stupid reality, unless, indeed, he becomes so brutalized that he understands nothing whatever.

What would he be like when I met him again? Still lively, witty, light-hearted and enthusiastic, or in a state of mental torpor induced by provincial life? A man may change greatly in the course of fifteen years!

The train stopped at a small station, and as I got out of the carriage, a stout, a very stout man with red cheeks and a big stomach rushed up to me with open arms, exclaiming: "George!" I embraced him, but I had not recognized him, and then I said, in astonishment: "By Jove! You have not grown thin!" And he replied with a laugh:

"What did you expect? Good living, a good table and good nights! Eating and sleeping, that is my existence!"

I looked at him closely, trying to discover in that broad face the features I held so dear. His eyes alone had not changed, but I no longer saw the same expression in them, and I said to myself: "If the expression be the reflection of the mind, the thoughts in that head are not what they used to be formerly; those thoughts which I knew so well."

Yet his eyes were bright, full of happiness and friendship, but they had not that clear, intelligent expression which shows as much as words the brightness of the intellect. Suddenly he said:

"Here are my two eldest children." A girl of fourteen, who was almost a woman, and a boy of thirteen, in the dress of a boy from a Lycee, came forward in a hesitating and awkward manner, and I said in a low voice: "Are they yours?" "Of course they are," he replied, laughing. "How many have you?" "Five! There are three more at home."

He said this in a proud, self-satisfied, almost triumphant manner, and I felt profound pity, mingled with a feeling of vague contempt, for this vainglorious and simple reproducer of his species.

I got into a carriage which he drove himself, and we set off through the town, a dull, sleepy, gloomy town where nothing was moving in the streets except a few dogs and two or three maidservants. Here and there a shopkeeper, standing at his door, took off his hat, and Simon returned his salute and told me the man's name; no doubt to show me that he knew all the inhabitants personally, and the thought struck me that he was thinking of becoming a candidate for the Chamber of Deputies, that dream of all those who bury themselves in the provinces.

We were soon out of the town, and the carriage turned into a garden that was an imitation of a park, and stopped in front of a turreted house, which tried to look like a chateau.

"That is my den," said Simon, so that I might compliment him on it. "It is charming," I replied.

A lady appeared on the steps, dressed for company, and with company phrases all ready prepared. She was no longer the light-haired, insipid girl I had seen in church fifteen years previously, but a stout lady in curls and flounces, one of those ladies of uncertain age, without intellect, without any of those things that go to make a woman. In short, she was a mother, a stout, commonplace mother, a human breeding machine which procreates without any other preoccupation but her children and her cook-book.

She welcomed me, and I went into the hall, where three children, ranged according to their height, seemed set out for review, like firemen before a mayor, and I said: "Ah! ah! so there are the others?" Simon, radiant with pleasure, introduced them: "Jean, Sophie and Gontran."

The door of the drawing-room was open. I went in, and in the depths of an easy-chair, I saw something trembling, a man, an old, paralyzed man. Madame Radevin came forward and said: "This is my grandfather, monsieur; he is eighty-seven." And then she shouted into the shaking old man's ears: "This is a friend of Simon's, papa." The old gentleman tried to say "good-day" to me, and he muttered: "Oua, oua, oua," and waved his hand, and I took a seat saying: "You are very kind, monsieur."

Simon had just come in, and he said with a laugh: "So! You have made grandpapa's acquaintance. He is a treasure, that old man; he is the delight of the children. But he is so greedy that he almost kills himself at every meal; you have no idea what he would eat if he were allowed to do as he pleased. But you will see, you will see. He looks at all the sweets as if they were so many girls. You never saw anything so funny; you will see presently."

I was then shown to my room, to change my dress for dinner, and hearing a great clatter behind me on the stairs, I turned round and saw that all the children were following me behind their father; to do me honor, no doubt.

My windows looked out across a dreary, interminable plain, an ocean of grass, of wheat and of oats, without a clump of trees or any rising ground, a striking and melancholy picture of the life which they must be leading in that house.

A bell rang; it was for dinner, and I went downstairs. Madame Radevin took my arm in a ceremonious manner, and we passed into the dining-room. A footman wheeled in the old man in his armchair. He gave a greedy and curious look at the dessert, as he turned his shaking head with difficulty from one dish to the other.

Simon rubbed his hands: "You will be amused," he said; and all the children understanding that I was going to be indulged with the sight of their greedy grandfather, began to laugh, while their mother merely smiled and shrugged her shoulders, and Simon, making a speaking trumpet of his hands, shouted at the old man: "This evening there is sweet creamed rice!" The wrinkled face of the grandfather brightened, and he trembled more violently, from head to foot, showing that he had understood and was very pleased. The dinner began.

"Just look!" Simon whispered. The old man did not like the soup, and refused to eat it; but he was obliged to do it for the good of his health, and the footman forced the spoon into his mouth, while the old man blew so energetically, so as not to swallow the soup, that it was scattered like a spray all over the table and over his neighbors. The children writhed with laughter at the spectacle, while their father, who was also amused, said: "Is not the old man comical?"

During the whole meal they were taken up solely with him. He devoured the dishes on the table with his eyes, and tried to seize them and pull them over to him with his trembling hands. They put them almost within his reach, to see his useless efforts, his trembling clutches at them, the piteous appeal of his whole nature, of his eyes, of his mouth and of his nose as he smelt them, and he slobbered on his table napkin with eagerness, while uttering inarticulate grunts. And the whole family was highly amused at this horrible and grotesque scene.

Then they put a tiny morsel on his plate, and he ate with feverish gluttony, in order to get something more as soon as possible, and when the sweetened rice was brought in, he nearly had a fit, and groaned with greediness, and Gontran called out to him:

"You have eaten too much already; you can have no more." And they pretended not to give him any. Then he began to cry; he cried and trembled more violently than ever, while all the children laughed. At last, however, they gave him his helping, a very small piece; and as he ate the first mouthful, he made a comical noise in his throat, and a movement with his neck as ducks do when they swallow too large a morsel, and when he had swallowed it, he began to stamp his feet, so as to get more.

I was seized with pity for this saddening and ridiculous Tantalus, and interposed on his behalf:

"Come, give him a little more rice!" But Simon replied: "Oh! no, my dear fellow, if he were to eat too much, it would harm him, at his age."

I held my tongue, and thought over those words. Oh, ethics! Oh, logic! Oh, wisdom! At his age! So they deprived him of his only remaining pleasure out of regard for his health! His health! What would he do with it, inert and trembling wreck that he was? They were taking care of his life, so they said. His life? How many days? Ten, twenty, fifty, or a hundred? Why? For his own sake? Or to preserve for some time longer the spectacle of his impotent greediness in the family.

There was nothing left for him to do in this life, nothing whatever. He had one single wish left, one sole pleasure; why not grant him that last solace until he died?

After we had played cards for a long time, I went up to my room and to bed; I was low-spirited and sad, sad, sad! and I sat at my window. Not a sound could be heard outside but the beautiful warbling of a bird in a tree, somewhere in the distance. No doubt the bird was singing in a low voice during the night, to lull his mate, who was asleep on her eggs. And I thought of my poor friend's five children, and pictured him to myself, snoring by the side of his ugly wife.

SUICIDES

To Georges Legrand.

Hardly a day goes by without our reading a news item like the following in some newspaper:

"On Wednesday night the people living in No. 40 Rue de——, were awakened by two successive shots. The explosions seemed to come from the apartment occupied by M. X——. The door was broken in and the man was found bathed in his blood, still holding in one hand the revolver with which he had taken his life.

"M. X——was fifty-seven years of age, enjoying a comfortable income, and had everything necessary to make him happy. No cause can be found for his action."

What terrible grief, what unknown suffering, hidden despair, secret wounds drive these presumably happy persons to suicide? We search, we imagine tragedies of love, we suspect financial troubles, and, as we never find anything definite, we apply to these deaths the word "mystery."

A letter found on the desk of one of these "suicides without cause," and written during his last night, beside his loaded revolver, has come into our hands. We deem it rather interesting. It reveals none of those great catastrophes which we always expect to find behind these acts of despair; but it shows us the slow succession of the little vexations of life, the disintegration of a lonely existence, whose dreams have disappeared; it gives the reason for these tragic ends, which only nervous and high-strung people can understand.

Here it is:

"It is midnight. When I have finished this letter I shall kill myself. Why? I shall attempt to give the reasons, not for those who may read these lines, but for myself, to kindle my waning courage, to impress upon myself the fatal necessity of this act which can, at best, be only deferred.

"I was brought up by simple-minded parents who were unquestioning believers. And I believed as they did.

"My dream lasted a long time. The last veil has just been torn from my eyes.

"During the last few years a strange change has been taking place within me. All the events of Life, which formerly had to me the glow of a beautiful sunset, are now fading away. The true meaning of things has appeared to me in its brutal reality; and the true reason for love has bred in me disgust even for this poetic sentiment: 'We are the eternal toys of foolish and charming illusions, which are always being renewed.'

"On growing older, I had become partly reconciled to the awful mystery of life, to the uselessness of effort; when the emptiness of everything appeared to me in a new light, this evening, after dinner.

"Formerly, I was happy! Everything pleased me: the passing women, the appearance of the streets, the place where I lived; and I even took an interest in the cut of my clothes. But the repetition of the same sights has had the result of filling my heart with weariness and disgust, just as one would feel were one to go every night to the same theatre.

"For the last thirty years I have been rising at the same hour; and, at the same restaurant, for thirty years, I have been eating at the same hours the same dishes brought me by different waiters.

"I have tried travel. The loneliness which one feels in strange places terrified me. I felt so alone, so small on the earth that I quickly started on my homeward journey.

"But here the unchanging expression of my furniture, which has stood for thirty years in the same place, the smell of my apartments (for, with time, each dwelling takes on a particular odor) each night, these and other things disgust me and make me sick of living thus.

"Everything repeats itself endlessly. The way in which I put my key in the lock, the place where I always find my matches, the first object which meets my eye when I enter the room, make me feel like jumping out of the window and putting an end to those monotonous events from which we can never escape.

"Each day, when I shave, I feel an inordinate desire to cut my throat; and my face, which I see in the little mirror, always the same, with soap on my cheeks, has several times made me weak from sadness.

"Now I even hate to be with people whom I used to meet with pleasure; I know them so well, I can tell just what they are going to say and what I am going to answer. Each brain is like a circus, where the same horse keeps circling around eternally. We must circle round always, around the same ideas, the same joys, the same pleasures, the same habits, the same beliefs, the same sensations of disgust.

"The fog was terrible this evening. It enfolded the boulevard, where the street lights were dimmed and looked like smoking candles. A heavier weight than usual oppressed me. Perhaps my digestion was bad.

"For good digestion is everything in life. It gives the inspiration to the artist, amorous desires to young people, clear ideas to thinkers, the joy of life to everybody, and it also allows one to eat heartily (which is one of the greatest pleasures). A sick stomach induces scepticism unbelief, nightmares and the desire for death. I have often noticed this fact. Perhaps I would not kill myself, if my digestion had been good this evening.

"When I sat down in the arm-chair where I have been sitting every day for thirty years, I glanced around me, and just then I was seized by such a terrible distress that I thought I must go mad.

"I tried to think of what I could do to run away from myself. Every occupation struck me as being worse even than inaction. Then I bethought me of putting my papers in order.

"For a long time I have been thinking of clearing out my drawers; for, for the last thirty years, I have been throwing my letters and bills pell-mell into the same desk, and this confusion has often caused me considerable trouble. But I feel such moral and physical laziness at the sole idea of putting anything in order that I have never had the courage to begin this tedious business.

"I therefore opened my desk, intending to choose among my old papers and destroy the majority of them.

"At first I was bewildered by this array of documents, yellowed by age, then I chose one.

"Oh! if you cherish life, never disturb the burial place of old letters!

"And if, perchance, you should, take the contents by the handful, close your eyes that you may not read a word, so that you may not recognize some forgotten handwriting which may plunge you suddenly into a sea of memories; carry these papers to the fire; and when they are in ashes, crush them to an invisible powder, or otherwise you are lost—just as I have been lost for an hour.

"The first letters which I read did not interest me greatly. They were recent, and came from living men whom I still meet quite often, and whose presence does not move me to any great extent. But all at once one envelope made me start. My name was traced on it in a large, bold handwriting; and suddenly tears came to my eyes. That letter was from my dearest friend, the companion of my youth, the confidant of my hopes; and he appeared before me so clearly, with his pleasant smile and his hand outstretched, that a cold shiver ran down my back. Yes, yes, the dead come back, for I saw him! Our memory is a more perfect world than the universe: it gives back life to those who no longer exist.

"With trembling hand and dimmed eyes I reread everything that he told me, and in my poor sobbing heart I felt a wound so painful that I began to groan as a man whose bones are slowly being crushed.

"Then I travelled over my whole life, just as one travels along a river. I recognized people, so long forgotten that I no longer knew their names. Their faces alone lived in me. In my mother's letters I saw again the old servants, the shape of our house and the little insignificant odds and ends which cling to our minds.

"Yes, I suddenly saw again all my mother's old gowns, the different styles which she adopted and the several ways in which she dressed her hair. She haunted me especially in a silk dress, trimmed with old lace; and I remembered something she said one day when she was wearing this dress. She said: 'Robert, my child, if you do not stand up straight you will be round-shouldered all your life.'

"Then, opening another drawer, I found myself face to face with memories of tender passions: a dancing-pump, a torn handkerchief, even a garter, locks of hair and dried flowers. Then the sweet romances of my life, whose living heroines are now white-haired, plunged me into the deep melancholy of things. Oh, the young brows where blond locks curl, the caress of the hands, the glance which speaks, the hearts which beat, that smile which promises the lips, those lips which promise the embrace! And the first kiss—that endless kiss which makes you close your eyes, which drowns all thought in the immeasurable joy of approaching possession!

"Taking these old pledges of former love in both my hands, I covered them with furious caresses, and in my soul, torn by these memories, I saw them each again at the hour of surrender; and I suffered a torture more cruel than all the tortures invented in all the fables about hell.

"One last letter remained. It was written by me and dictated fifty years ago by my writing teacher. Here it is:

"'MY DEAR LITTLE MAMMA:

"'I am seven years old to-day. It is the age of reason. I take advantage of it to thank you for having brought me into this world.

"'Your little son, who loves you

"'ROBERT.'

"It is all over. I had gone back to the beginning, and suddenly I turned my glance on what remained to me of life. I saw hideous and lonely old age, and approaching infirmities, and everything over and gone. And nobody near me!

"My revolver is here, on the table. I am loading it . . . . Never reread your old letters!"

And that is how many men come to kill themselves; and we search in vain to discover some great sorrow in their lives.

AN ARTIFICE

The old doctor sat by the fireside, talking to his fair patient who was lying on the lounge. There was nothing much the matter with her, except that she had one of those little feminine ailments from which pretty women frequently suffer—slight anaemia, a nervous attack, etc.

"No, doctor," she said; "I shall never be able to understand a woman deceiving her husband. Even allowing that she does not love him, that she pays no heed to her vows and promises, how can she give herself to another man? How can she conceal the intrigue from other people's eyes? How can it be possible to love amid lies and treason?"

The doctor smiled, and replied: "It is perfectly easy, and I can assure you that a woman does not think of all those little subtle details when she has made up her mind to go astray.

"As for dissimulation, all women have plenty of it on hand for such occasions, and the simplest of them are wonderful, and extricate themselves from the greatest dilemmas in a remarkable manner."

The young woman, however, seemed incredulous.

"No, doctor," she said; "one never thinks until after it has happened of what one ought to have done in a critical situation, and women are certainly more liable than men to lose their head on such occasions:"

The doctor raised his hands. "After it has happened, you say! Now I will tell you something that happened to one of my female patients, whom I always considered an immaculate woman.

"It happened in a provincial town, and one night when I was asleep, in that deep first sleep from which it is so difficult to rouse us, it seemed to me, in my dreams, as if the bells in the town were sounding a fire alarm, and I woke up with a start. It was my own bell, which was ringing wildly, and as my footman did not seem to be answering the door, I, in turn, pulled the bell at the head of my bed, and soon I heard a banging, and steps in the silent house, and Jean came into my room, and handed me a letter which said:

'Madame Lelievre begs Dr. Simeon to come to her immediately.'

"I thought for a few moments, and then I said to myself: 'A nervous attack, vapors; nonsense, I am too tired.' And so I replied: 'As Dr. Simeon is not at all well, he must beg Madame Lelievre to be kind enough to call in his colleague, Monsieur Bonnet.' I put the note into an envelope and went to sleep again, but about half an hour later the street bell rang again, and Jean came to me and said: 'There is somebody downstairs; I do not quite know whether it is a man or a woman, as the individual is so wrapped up, but they wish to speak to you immediately. They say it is a matter of life and death for two people.' Whereupon I sat up in bed and told him to show the person in.

"A kind of black phantom appeared and raised her veil as soon as Jean had left the room. It was Madame Berthe Lelievre, quite a young woman, who had been married for three years to a large merchant in the town, who was said to have married the prettiest girl in the neighborhood.

"She was terribly pale, her face was contracted as the faces of insane people are, occasionally, and her hands trembled violently. Twice she tried to speak without being able to utter a sound, but at last she stammered out: 'Come—quick—quick, doctor. Come—my—friend has just died in my bedroom.' She stopped, half suffocated with emotion, and then went on: 'My husband will be coming home from the club very soon.'

"I jumped out of bed without even considering that I was only in my nightshirt, and dressed myself in a few moments, and then I said: 'Did you come a short time ago?' 'No,' she said, standing like a statue petrified with horror. 'It was my servant—she knows.' And then, after a short silence, she went on: 'I was there—by his side.' And she uttered a sort of cry of horror, and after a fit of choking, which made her gasp, she wept violently, and shook with spasmodic sobs for a minute: or two. Then her tears suddenly ceased, as if by an internal fire, and with an air of tragic calmness, she said: 'Let us make haste.'

"I was ready, but exclaimed: 'I quite forgot to order my carriage.' 'I have one,' she said; 'it is his, which was waiting for him!' She wrapped herself up, so as to completely conceal her face, and we started.

"When she was by my side in the carriage she suddenly seized my hand, and crushing it in her delicate fingers, she said, with a shaking voice, that proceeded from a distracted heart: 'Oh! if you only knew, if you only knew what I am suffering! I loved him, I have loved him distractedly, like a madwoman, for the last six months.' 'Is anyone up in your house?' I asked. 'No, nobody except those, who knows everything.'

"We stopped at the door, and evidently everybody was asleep. We went in without making any noise, by means of her latch-key, and walked upstairs on tiptoe. The frightened servant was sitting on the top of the stairs with a lighted candle by her side, as she was afraid to remain with the dead man, and I went into the room, which was in great disorder. Wet towels, with which they had bathed the young man's temples, were lying on the floor, by the side of a washbasin and a glass, while a strong smell of vinegar pervaded the room.

"The dead man's body was lying at full length in the middle of the room, and I went up to it, looked at it, and touched it. I opened the eyes and felt the hands, and then, turning to the two women, who were shaking as if they were freezing, I said to them: 'Help me to lift him on to the bed.' When we had laid him gently on it, I listened to his heart and put a looking-glass to his lips, and then said: 'It is all over.' It was a terrible sight!

"I looked at the man, and said: 'You ought to arrange his hair a little.' The girl went and brought her mistress' comb and brush, but as she was trembling, and pulling out his long, matted hair in doing it, Madame Lelievre took the comb out of her hand, and arranged his hair as if she were caressing him. She parted it, brushed his beard, rolled his mustaches gently round her fingers, then, suddenly, letting go of his hair, she took the dead man's inert head in her hands and looked for a long time in despair at the dead face, which no longer could smile at her, and then, throwing herself on him, she clasped him in her arms and kissed him ardently. Her kisses fell like blows on his closed mouth and eyes, his forehead and temples; and then, putting her lips to his ear, as if he could still hear her, and as if she were about to whisper something to him, she said several times, in a heartrending voice:

"'Good-by, my darling!'

"Just then the clock struck twelve, and I started up. 'Twelve o'clock!' I exclaimed. 'That is the time when the club closes. Come, madame, we have not a moment to lose!' She started up, and I said:

"'We must carry him into the drawing-room.' And when we had done this, I placed him on a sofa, and lit the chandeliers, and just then the front door was opened and shut noisily. 'Rose, bring me the basin and the towels, and make the room look tidy. Make haste, for Heaven's sake! Monsieur Lelievre is coming in.'

"I heard his steps on the stairs, and then his hands feeling along the walls. 'Come here, my dear fellow,' I said; 'we have had an accident.'

"And the astonished husband appeared in the door with a cigar in his mouth, and said: 'What is the matter? What is the meaning of this?' 'My dear friend,' I said, going up to him, 'you find us in great embarrassment. I had remained late, chatting with your wife and our friend, who had brought me in his carriage, when he suddenly fainted, and in spite of all we have done, he has remained unconscious for two hours. I did not like to call in strangers, and if you will now help me downstairs with him, I shall be able to attend to him better at his own house.'

"The husband, who was surprised, but quite unsuspicious, took off his hat, and then he took his rival, who would be quite inoffensive for the future, under the arms. I got between his two legs, as if I had been a horse between the shafts, and we went downstairs, while his wife held a light for us. When we got outside I stood the body up, so as to deceive the coachman, and said: 'Come, my friend; it is nothing; you feel better already I expect. Pluck up your courage, and make an effort. It will soon be over.' But as I felt that he was slipping out of my hands, I gave him a slap on the shoulder, which sent him forward and made him fall into the carriage, and then I got in after him. Monsieur Lelievre, who was rather alarmed, said to me: 'Do you think it is anything serious?' To which I replied: 'No,' with a smile, as I looked at his wife, who had put her arm into that of her husband, and was trying to see into the carriage.

"I shook hands with them and told my coachman to start, and during the whole drive the dead man kept falling against me. When we got to his house I said that he had become unconscious on the way home, and helped to carry him upstairs, where I certified that he was dead, and acted another comedy to his distracted family, and at last I got back to bed, not without swearing at lovers."

The doctor ceased, though he was still smiling, and the young woman, who was in a very nervous state, said: "Why have you told me that terrible story?"

He gave her a gallant bow, and replied:

"So that I may offer you my services if they should be needed."

DREAMS

They had just dined together, five old friends, a writer, a doctor and three rich bachelors without any profession.

They had talked about everything, and a feeling of lassitude came over them, that feeling which precedes and leads to the departure of guests after festive gatherings. One of those present, who had for the last five minutes been gazing silently at the surging boulevard dotted with gas-lamps, with its rattling vehicles, said suddenly:

"When you've nothing to do from morning till night, the days are long."

"And the nights too," assented the guest who sat next to him. "I sleep very little; pleasures fatigue me; conversation is monotonous. Never do I come across a new idea, and I feel, before talking to any one, a violent longing to say nothing and to listen to nothing. I don't know what to do with my evenings."

The third idler remarked:

"I would pay a great deal for anything that would help me to pass just two pleasant hours every day."

The writer, who had just thrown his overcoat across his arm, turned round to them, and said:

"The man who could discover a new vice and introduce it among his fellow creatures, even if it were to shorten their lives, would render a greater service to humanity than the man who found the means of securing to them eternal salvation and eternal youth."

The doctor burst out laughing, and, while he chewed his cigar, he said:

"Yes, but it is not so easy to discover it. Men have however crudely, been seeking for—and working for the object you refer to since the beginning of the world. The men who came first reached perfection at once in this way. We are hardly equal to them."

One of the three idlers murmured:

"What a pity!"

Then, after a minute's pause, he added:

"If we could only sleep, sleep well, without feeling hot or cold, sleep with that perfect unconsciousness we experience on nights when we are thoroughly fatigued, sleep without dreams."

"Why without dreams?" asked the guest sitting next to him.

The other replied:

"Because dreams are not always pleasant; they are always fantastic, improbable, disconnected; and because when we are asleep we cannot have the sort of dreams we like. We ought to dream waking."

"And what's to prevent you?" asked the writer.

The doctor flung away the end of his cigar.

"My dear fellow, in order to dream when you are awake, you need great power and great exercise of will, and when you try to do it, great weariness is the result. Now, real dreaming, that journey of our thoughts through delightful visions, is assuredly the sweetest experience in the world; but it must come naturally, it must not be provoked in a painful, manner, and must be accompanied by absolute bodily comfort. This power of dreaming I can give you, provided you promise that you will not abuse it."

The writer shrugged his shoulders:

"Ah! yes, I know—hasheesh, opium, green tea—artificial paradises. I have read Baudelaire, and I even tasted the famous drug, which made me very sick."

But the doctor, without stirring from his seat, said:

"No; ether, nothing but ether; and I would suggest that you literary men should use it sometimes."

The three rich bachelors drew closer to the doctor.

One of them said:

"Explain to us the effects of it."

And the doctor replied:

"Let us put aside big words, shall we not? I am not talking of medicine or morality; I am talking of pleasure. You give yourselves up every day to excesses which consume your lives. I want to indicate to you a new sensation, possible only to intelligent men—let us say even very intelligent men—dangerous, like everything else that overexcites our organs, but exquisite. I might add that you would require a certain preparation, that is to say, practice, to feel in all their completeness the singular effects of ether.

"They are different from the effects of hasheesh, of opium, or morphia, and they cease as soon as the absorption of the drug is interrupted, while the other generators of day dreams continue their action for hours.

"I am now going to try to analyze these feelings as clearly as possible. But the thing is not easy, so facile, so delicate, so almost imperceptible, are these sensations.

"It was when I was attacked by violent neuralgia that I made use of this remedy, which since then I have, perhaps, slightly abused.

"I had acute pains in my head and neck, and an intolerable heat of the skin, a feverish restlessness. I took up a large bottle of ether, and, lying down, I began to inhale it slowly.

"At the end of some minutes I thought I heard a vague murmur, which ere long became a sort of humming, and it seemed to me that all the interior of my body had become light, light as air, that it was dissolving into vapor.

"Then came a sort of torpor, a sleepy sensation of comfort, in spite of the pains which still continued, but which had ceased to make themselves felt. It was one of those sensations which we are willing to endure and not any of those frightful wrenches against which our tortured body protests.

"Soon the strange and delightful sense of emptiness which I felt in my chest extended to my limbs, which, in their turn, became light, as light as if the flesh and the bones had been melted and the skin only were left, the skin necessary to enable me to realize the sweetness of living, of bathing in this sensation of well-being. Then I perceived that I was no longer suffering. The pain had gone, melted away, evaporated. And I heard voices, four voices, two dialogues, without understanding what was said. At one time there were only indistinct sounds, at another time a word reached my ear. But I recognized that this was only the humming I had heard before, but emphasized. I was not asleep; I was not awake; I comprehended, I felt, I reasoned with the utmost clearness and depth, with extraordinary energy and intellectual pleasure, with a singular intoxication arising from this separation of my mental faculties.

"It was not like the dreams caused by hasheesh or the somewhat sickly visions that come from opium; it was an amazing acuteness of reasoning, a new way of seeing, judging and appreciating the things of life, and with the certainty, the absolute consciousness that this was the true way.

"And the old image of the Scriptures suddenly came back to my mind. It seemed to me that I had tasted of the Tree of Knowledge, that all the mysteries were unveiled, so much did I find myself under the sway of a new, strange and irrefutable logic. And arguments, reasonings, proofs rose up in a heap before my brain only to be immediately displaced by some stronger proof, reasoning, argument. My head had, in fact, become a battleground of ideas.

I was a superior being, armed with invincible intelligence, and I experienced a huge delight at the manifestation of my power.

"It lasted a long, long time. I still kept inhaling the ether from my flagon. Suddenly I perceived that it was empty."

The four men exclaimed at the same time:

"Doctor, a prescription at once for a liter of ether!"

But the doctor, putting on his hat, replied:

"As to that, certainly not; go and let some one else poison you!"

And he left them.

Ladies and gentlemen, what is your opinion on the subject?

SIMON'S PAPA

Noon had just struck. The school door opened and the youngsters darted out, jostling each other in their haste to get out quickly. But instead of promptly dispersing and going home to dinner as usual, they stopped a few paces off, broke up into knots, and began whispering.

The fact was that, that morning, Simon, the son of La Blanchotte, had, for the first time, attended school.

They had all of them in their families heard talk of La Blanchotte; and, although in public she was welcome enough, the mothers among themselves treated her with a somewhat disdainful compassion, which the children had imitated without in the least knowing why.

As for Simon himself, they did not know him, for he never went out, and did not run about with them in the streets of the village, or along the banks of the river. And they did not care for him; so it was with a certain delight, mingled with considerable astonishment, that they met and repeated to each other what had been said by a lad of fourteen or fifteen who appeared to know all about it, so sagaciously did he wink. "You know—Simon—well, he has no papa."

Just then La Blanchotte's son appeared in the doorway of the school.

He was seven or eight years old, rather pale, very neat, with a timid and almost awkward manner.

He was starting home to his mother's house when the groups of his schoolmates, whispering and watching him with the mischievous and heartless eyes of children bent upon playing a nasty trick, gradually closed in around him and ended by surrounding him altogether. There he stood in their midst, surprised and embarrassed, not understanding what they were going to do with him. But the lad who had brought the news, puffed up with the success he had met with already, demanded:

"What is your name, you?"

He answered: "Simon."

"Simon what?" retorted the other.

The child, altogether bewildered, repeated: "Simon."

The lad shouted at him: "One is named Simon something—that is not a name—Simon indeed."

The child, on the brink of tears, replied for the third time:

"My name is Simon."

The urchins began to laugh. The triumphant tormentor cried: "You can see plainly that he has no papa."

A deep silence ensued. The children were dumfounded by this extraordinary, impossible, monstrous thing—a boy who had not a papa; they looked upon him as a phenomenon, an unnatural being, and they felt that hitherto inexplicable contempt of their mothers for La Blanchotte growing upon them. As for Simon, he had leaned against a tree to avoid falling, and he remained as if prostrated by an irreparable disaster. He sought to explain, but could think of nothing-to say to refute this horrible charge that he had no papa. At last he shouted at them quite recklessly: "Yes, I have one."

"Where is he?" demanded the boy.

Simon was silent, he did not know. The children roared, tremendously excited; and those country boys, little more than animals, experienced that cruel craving which prompts the fowls of a farmyard to destroy one of their number as soon as it is wounded. Simon suddenly espied a little neighbor, the son of a widow, whom he had seen, as he himself was to be seen, always alone with his mother.

"And no more have you," he said; "no more have you a papa."

"Yes," replied the other, "I have one."

"Where is he?" rejoined Simon.

"He is dead," declared the brat, with superb dignity; "he is in the cemetery, is my papa."

A murmur of approval rose among the little wretches as if this fact of possessing a papa dead in a cemetery had caused their comrade to grow big enough to crush the other one who had no papa at all. And these boys, whose fathers were for the most part bad men, drunkards, thieves, and who beat their wives, jostled each other to press closer and closer, as though they, the legitimate ones, would smother by their pressure one who was illegitimate.

The boy who chanced to be next Simon suddenly put his tongue out at him with a mocking air and shouted at him:

"No papa! No papa!"

Simon seized him by the hair with both hands and set to work to disable his legs with kicks, while he bit his cheek ferociously. A tremendous struggle ensued between the two combatants, and Simon found himself beaten, torn, bruised, rolled on the ground in the midst of the ring of applauding schoolboys. As he arose, mechanically brushing with his hand his little blouse all covered with dust, some one shouted at him:

"Go and tell your papa."

Then he felt a great sinking at his heart. They were stronger than he was, they had beaten him, and he had no answer to give them, for he knew well that it was true that he had no papa. Full of pride, he attempted for some moments to struggle against the tears which were choking him. He had a feeling of suffocation, and then without any sound he commenced to weep, with great shaking sobs. A ferocious joy broke out among his enemies, and, with one accord, just like savages in their fearful festivals, they took each other by the hand and danced round him in a circle, repeating as a refrain:

"No papa! No papa!"

But suddenly Simon ceased sobbing. He became ferocious. There were stones under his feet; he picked them up and with all his strength hurled them at his tormentors. Two or three were struck and rushed off yelling, and so formidable did he appear that the rest became panic-stricken. Cowards, as the mob always is in presence of an exasperated man, they broke up and fled. Left alone, the little fellow without a father set off running toward the fields, for a recollection had been awakened in him which determined his soul to a great resolve. He made up his mind to drown himself in the river.

He remembered, in fact, that eight days before, a poor devil who begged for his livelihood had thrown himself into the water because he had no more money. Simon had been there when they fished him out again; and the wretched man, who usually seemed to him so miserable, and ugly, had then struck him as being so peaceful with his pale cheeks, his long drenched beard, and his open eyes full of calm. The bystanders had said:

"He is dead."

And some one had said:

"He is quite happy now."

And Simon wished to drown himself also, because he had no father, just like the wretched being who had no money.

He reached the water and watched it flowing. Some fish were sporting briskly in the clear stream and occasionally made a little bound and caught the flies flying on the surface. He stopped crying in order to watch them, for their maneuvers interested him greatly. But, at intervals, as in a tempest intervals of calm alternate suddenly with tremendous gusts of wind, which snap off the trees and then lose themselves in the horizon, this thought would return to him with intense pain:

"I am going to drown myself because I have no papa."

It was very warm, fine weather. The pleasant sunshine warmed the grass. The water shone like a mirror. And Simon enjoyed some minutes of happiness, of that languor which follows weeping, and felt inclined to fall asleep there upon the grass in the warm sunshine.

A little green frog leaped from under his feet. He endeavored to catch it. It escaped him. He followed it and lost it three times in succession. At last he caught it by one of its hind legs and began to laugh as he saw the efforts the creature made to escape. It gathered itself up on its hind legs and then with a violent spring suddenly stretched them out as stiff as two bars; while it beat the air with its front legs as though they were hands, its round eyes staring in their circle of yellow. It reminded him of a toy made of straight slips of wood nailed zigzag one on the other; which by a similar movement regulated the movements of the little soldiers fastened thereon. Then he thought of his home, and then of his mother, and, overcome by sorrow, he again began to weep. A shiver passed over him. He knelt down and said his prayers as before going to bed. But he was unable to finish them, for tumultuous, violent sobs shook his whole frame. He no longer thought, he no longer saw anything around him, and was wholly absorbed in crying.

Suddenly a heavy hand was placed upon his shoulder, and a rough voice asked him:

"What is it that causes you so much grief, my little man?"

Simon turned round. A tall workman with a beard and black curly hair was staring at him good-naturedly. He answered with his eyes and throat full of tears:

"They beat me—because—I—I have no—papa—no papa."

"What!" said the man, smiling; "why, everybody has one."

The child answered painfully amid his spasms of grief:

"But I—I—I have none."

Then the workman became serious. He had recognized La Blanchotte's son, and, although himself a new arrival in the neighborhood, he had a vague idea of her history.

"Well," said he, "console yourself, my boy, and come with me home to your mother. They will give you—a papa."

And so they started on the way, the big fellow holding the little fellow by the hand, and the man smiled, for he was not sorry to see this Blanchotte, who was, it was said, one of the prettiest girls of the countryside, and, perhaps, he was saying to himself, at the bottom of his heart, that a lass who had erred might very well err again.

They arrived in front of a very neat little white house.

"There it is," exclaimed the child, and he cried, "Mamma!"

A woman appeared, and the workman instantly left off smiling, for he saw at once that there was no fooling to be done with the tall pale girl who stood austerely at her door as though to defend from one man the threshold of that house where she had already been betrayed by another. Intimidated, his cap in his hand, he stammered out:

"See, madame, I have brought you back your little boy who had lost himself near the river."

But Simon flung his arms about his mother's neck and told her, as he again began to cry:

"No, mamma, I wished to drown myself, because the others had beaten me —had beaten me—because I have no papa."

A burning redness covered the young woman's cheeks; and, hurt to the quick, she embraced her child passionately, while the tears coursed down her face. The man, much moved, stood there, not knowing how to get away.

But Simon suddenly ran to him and said:

"Will you be my papa?"

A deep silence ensued. La Blanchotte, dumb and tortured with shame, leaned herself against the wall, both her hands upon her heart. The child, seeing that no answer was made him, replied:

"If you will not, I shall go back and drown myself."

The workman took the matter as a jest and answered, laughing:

"Why, yes, certainly I will."

"What is your name," went on the child, "so that I may tell the others when they wish to know your name?"

"Philip," answered the man:

Simon was silent a moment so that he might get the name well into his head; then he stretched out his arms, quite consoled, as he said:

"Well, then, Philip, you are my papa."

The workman, lifting him from the ground, kissed him hastily on both cheeks, and then walked away very quickly with great strides. When the child returned to school next day he was received with a spiteful laugh, and at the end of school, when the lads were on the point of recommencing, Simon threw these words at their heads as he would have done a stone: "He is named Philip, my papa."

Yells of delight burst out from all sides.

"Philip who? Philip what? What on earth is Philip? Where did you pick up your Philip?"

Simon answered nothing; and, immovable in his faith, he defied them with his eye, ready to be martyred rather than fly before them. The school master came to his rescue and he returned home to his mother.

During three months, the tall workman, Philip, frequently passed by La Blanchotte's house, and sometimes he made bold to speak to her when he saw her sewing near the window. She answered him civilly, always sedately, never joking with him, nor permitting him to enter her house. Notwithstanding, being, like all men, a bit of a coxcomb, he imagined that she was often rosier than usual when she chatted with him.

But a lost reputation is so difficult to regain and always remains so fragile that, in spite of the shy reserve of La Blanchotte, they already gossiped in the neighborhood.

As for Simon he loved his new papa very much, and walked with him nearly every evening when the day's work was done. He went regularly to school, and mixed with great dignity with his schoolfellows without ever answering them back.

One day, however, the lad who had first attacked him said to him:

"You have lied. You have not a papa named Philip."

"Why do you say that?" demanded Simon, much disturbed.

The youth rubbed his hands. He replied:

"Because if you had one he would be your mamma's husband."

Simon was confused by the truth of this reasoning; nevertheless, he retorted:

"He is my papa, all the same."

"That can very well be," exclaimed the urchin with a sneer, "but that is not being your papa altogether."

La Blanchotte's little one bowed his head and went off dreaming in the direction of the forge belonging to old Loizon, where Philip worked. This forge was as though buried beneath trees. It was very dark there; the red glare of a formidable furnace alone lit up with great flashes five blacksmiths; who hammered upon their anvils with a terrible din. They were standing enveloped in flame, like demons, their eyes fixed on the red-hot iron they were pounding; and their dull ideas rose and fell with their hammers.

Simon entered without being noticed, and went quietly to pluck his friend by the sleeve. The latter turned round. All at once the work came to a standstill, and all the men looked on, very attentive. Then, in the midst of this unaccustomed silence, rose the slender pipe of Simon:

"Say, Philip, the Michaude boy told me just now that you were not altogether my papa."

"Why not?" asked the blacksmith,

The child replied with all innocence:

"Because you are not my mamma's husband."

No one laughed. Philip remained standing, leaning his forehead upon the back of his great hands, which supported the handle of his hammer standing upright upon the anvil. He mused. His four companions watched him, and Simon, a tiny mite among these giants, anxiously waited. Suddenly, one of the smiths, answering to the sentiment of all, said to Philip:

"La Blanchotte is a good, honest girl, and upright and steady in spite of her misfortune, and would make a worthy wife for an honest man."

"That is true," remarked the three others.

The smith continued:

"Is it the girl's fault if she went wrong? She had been promised marriage; and I know more than one who is much respected today, and who sinned every bit as much."

"That is true," responded the three men in chorus.

He resumed:

"How hard she has toiled, poor thing, to bring up her child all alone, and how she has wept all these years she has never gone out except to church, God only knows."

"This is also true," said the others.

Then nothing was heard but the bellows which fanned the fire of the furnace. Philip hastily bent himself down to Simon:

"Go and tell your mother that I am coming to speak to her this evening." Then he pushed the child out by the shoulders. He returned to his work, and with a single blow the five hammers again fell upon their anvils. Thus they wrought the iron until nightfall, strong, powerful, happy, like contented hammers. But just as the great bell of a cathedral resounds upon feast days above the jingling of the other bells, so Philip's hammer, sounding above the rest, clanged second after second with a deafening uproar. And he stood amid the flying sparks plying his trade vigorously.

The sky was full of stars as he knocked at La Blanchotte's door. He had on his Sunday blouse, a clean shirt, and his beard was trimmed. The young woman showed herself upon the threshold, and said in a grieved tone:

"It is ill to come thus when night has fallen, Mr. Philip."

He wished to answer, but stammered and stood confused before her.

She resumed:

"You understand, do you not, that it will not do for me to be talked about again."

"What does that matter to me, if you will be my wife!"

No voice replied to him, but he believed that he heard in the shadow of the room the sound of a falling body. He entered quickly; and Simon, who had gone to bed, distinguished the sound of a kiss and some words that his mother murmured softly. Then, all at once, he found himself lifted up by the hands of his friend, who, holding him at the length of his herculean arms, exclaimed:

"You will tell them, your schoolmates, that your papa is Philip Remy, the blacksmith, and that he will pull the ears of all who do you any harm."

On the morrow, when the school was full and lessons were about to begin, little Simon stood up, quite pale with trembling lips:

"My papa," said he in a clear voice, "is Philip Remy, the blacksmith, and he has promised to pull the ears of all who does me any harm."

This time no one laughed, for he was very well known, was Philip Remy, the blacksmith, and was a papa of whom any one in the world would have been proud.

CPSIA information can be obtained
at www.ICGtesting.com
Printed in the USA
LVHW041821140720
660698LV00025B/682

9 781641 817493